Our Stories, Our Songs

Published in Canada by Fitzhenry & Whiteside, 195 Allstate Parkway, Markham, Ontario L3R 4T8

Published in the United States by Fitzhenry & Whiteside, 121 Harvard Avenue, Suite 2, Allston, Massachusetts 02134

www.fitzhenry.ca   godwit@fitzhenry.ca

10 9 8 7 6 5 4 3 2 1

Library and Archives Canada Cataloguing in Publication

Ellis, Deborah, 1960-
    Our stories, our songs / Deborah Ellis.

ISBN 1-55041-913-7 (bound).–ISBN 1-55041-912-9 (pbk.)

    1. Children of AIDS patients—Tanzania—Juvenile literature.
2. Children of AIDS patients—Malawi—Juvenile literature. 3. Orphans-
Tanzania-Juvenile literature. 4. Orphans-Malawi-Juvenile literature.
5. Children–Tanzania-Social conditions-Juvenile literature.
6. Children—Malawi—Social conditions-Juvenile literature. I. Title.

RA643.86.A35E44 2005   j362.7'09678   C2005-902890-4

U.S. Publisher Cataloging-in-Publication Data (Library of Congress Standards)

Ellis, Deborah.
    Our stories, our songs / Deborah Ellis.
[256] p. : cm.
Summary: In Malawi and Tanzania, children who have lost family to the AIDS pandemic tell their stories.
ISBN 1-55041-913-7
ISBN 1-55041-912-9 (pbk)
1. Children of AIDS patients – Malawi — Juvenile literature. 2. Children of AIDS patients —
Tanzanian — Juvenile literature. 3. AIDS (Disease) — Malawi — Literary collections — Juvenile literature. 4. AIDS (Disease) — Tanzanian — Literary collections — Juvenile literature. I. Title.
362.1/969792/0096 dc22   RA643.86.A357E55 2005

Fitzhenry & Whiteside acknowledges with thanks the Canada Council for the Arts, the Government of Canada through the Book Publishing Industry Development Program (BPIDP), and the Ontario Arts Council for their support of our publishing program.

Design by Fortunato Design Inc.

Photo Credits: cover—courtesy of the Friends of Mulanje Orphans; all interior photos supplied by the author except for pp. 13, 51, 101, 102, and 103—courtesy of the Friends of Mulanje Orphans

Printed in Canada

Our Stories, Our Songs:

African Children Talk About AIDS

By Deborah Ellis

Fitzhenry & Whiteside

My life flows on in endless song
Above Earth's lamentation.
I hear the ringing far off hymn
That hails a new creation.
No storm can shake my inmost calm
While to that rock I'm clinging
It sounds an echo in my soul
How can I keep from singing?

—PETE SEEGER,
American folk musician and songwriter

Table of Contents

Introduction / vii

PART ONE:
Songs At The Edge / 1

LIFE IN CHOWOMBA / 2

BOUNCED AROUND / 8

NEW DESKS / 11

THE ISLAND IN THE SKY / 16

ON THE STREET / 25

TROUBLE / 34

PRISON / 38

BABIES / 45

PART TWO:
Songs of Survival / 49

BEING SICK / 49

PEER COUNSELING / 53

LIVING / 59

PART THREE:
Songs of Victory / 67

ANTI-AIDS CLUBS / 73

KICKING AIDS OUT / 75

ARTS AGAINST AIDS / 79

STORY WORKSHOP / 90

Conclusion / 95

WHAT AIDS IS AND WHAT IT DOES / 96

HOW TO CATCH AIDS / 97

HOW NOT TO CATCH AIDS / 97

AIDS AROUND THE WORLD / 98

AIDS TERMS / 99

MAP / 100

RESOURCES / 101

Index / 102

About the Author / 104

Introduction

AIDS (Acquired Immunodeficiency Syndrome) has orphaned 11.5 million children in Sub-Saharan Africa. That number is expected to rise to 20 million by the year 2020.

These numbers tell us how bad the crisis is, but numbers don't tell us much about the people caught up in this crisis. As an author, I write in order to find out about the world. I wanted to know what it really means to be a child living in the midst of this terrible pandemic. In order to find out, I traveled to Malawi and Zambia in the summer of 2003 and met some of these children. This book is the result of that trip.

This was my first visit to the continent of Africa. I stayed in hostels and people's homes, traveled on crowded public minibuses, got lost a lot, and made more than a few mistakes. I was often sad, sometimes scared, and always acutely aware of how privileged I was to be able to travel and learn from people who are living with such monumental struggles.

Before leaving Canada, I had made contact with some people in Malawi and Zambia via the Internet. Some of these contacts worked out; some fell through, quite possibly because I couldn't figure out how to use the telephones there. A lot of the stories in this book came from people I met by chance along the street. AIDS has affected everyone. Everyone has a story.

The children I met are awe-inspiring. They welcomed me into their lives. Gracious and generous, they answered very personal questions about life and death put to them by a stranger. Some of the interviews I did were conducted in English; some were conducted in the local languages through interpreters.

AIDS has touched all the children you will meet in these pages. Many are orphans who looked after their dying parents and are now raising younger brothers and sisters. Some live on the street. Some are in prison. Some are artists and activists who raise their voices for justice and dignity.

I stepped into this pandemic rather late. It has been raging since the 1980s. A whole generation has come of age with this disease clouding their futures. I expected to find mourning, fear, and death—and I did find those things. But I also found courage, celebration, community, and the determination of people getting on with the business of life.

As I've seen in other places in the world, human beings have an enormous capacity for cruelty—and for kindness. Certainly in the world of AIDS, both exist. AIDS has combined with other factors to create widespread poverty. Desperate poverty can drive people to do desperate things, especially when there is no end in sight. Desperate poverty can also inspire people to stupendous acts of courage, such as welcoming into their home more children than they can feed and then, somehow, finding food for them.

To be an AIDS orphan is to face discrimination. It can mean being shunned by people who don't know that AIDS is not spread by casual contact. To be an AIDS orphan usually means living in poverty, having to leave school, being abused by unfair employers, and being put at risk by adults who ought to know better.

We all need to believe that our lives have meaning, that our existence is acknowledged, and that we are valued. AIDS challenges all of us. We can meet that challenge by embracing the sufferers and assisting the survivors to lead lives of dignity and hope.

The children of AIDS have long roads ahead of them. It is a privilege for all of us to walk those roads with them, and to do what we can to lighten their load.

PART ONE:
Songs At The Edge

We need to remind ourselves why so many children are orphans today: because their parents were not able to get treatment for AIDS, most likely because they could not afford it, or because they lived in a country which was too poor to provide their basic health care. We must know that one of the greatest assaults to human dignity is poverty, where you wake up not knowing where you're going to get your next meal. When you cannot have decent accommodation for yourself and your children. When you cannot feed them, and send them to school. That is the greatest assault on human dignity.

—NELSON MANDELA
Former president, South Africa

POVERTY

- The 200 richest people in the world have more money than the poorest 582,000,000 people combined.

- One-sixth of the people in the world are malnourished.

- Between 1985 and 2000, over 7 million African farmers died of AIDS.

- Most African countries pay up to three times more on international debt repayment than they do on health care.

- Hunger weakens the body, making it vulnerable to illness. This makes it harder to stay strong if someone is HIV-positive.

- HIV infection rates are rising among African American and Hispanic people living in poverty.

- Living in poverty forces people to make unsafe choices in order to survive or feed their children.

- Most of the 42 million people with HIV/AIDS live in countries with a lot of poverty, 29 million in Sub-Saharan Africa.

- It costs more to care for and bury someone with AIDS than most rural African families earn in a year.

1

LIFE IN CHOWOMBA

Lusaka is the capital city of Zambia. One million of Zambia's 10 million people live here. The downtown has high office towers, wide tree-lined streets, and many shops.

Chowomba is a congested, low-income neighborhood on the outskirts of Lusaka. Small mud-brick and tin-roof houses crowd together off narrow dirt roads and pathways. Minibuses overflowing with people drive among roadside stands where merchants sell a few vegetables displayed on pieces of cardboard on the ground.

On the sidewalk outside the post office, I meet Agnes. She asks me to buy one of her red ribbons, with the money going to support AIDS orphans. We start talking and she invites me to her home to meet some of the children she takes care of.

I meet Collins and his friends in the small, dark shed where he lives with his mother Agnes and many other children. It is a chilly day. A bit of coal is burning on a small brazier on the bare cement floor of the shed.

COLLINS, 8

Nothing scares me.

I don't remember very much about when my father died. I was quite small, and you don't always remember what happens to you when you're small. I think he suffered from bad headaches, and also he ran out of blood. When he was well, he was very kind to me and would let me ride on his shoulders, or just let me sit beside him while he talked to other men.

He was a soldier. He was very strong, when he wasn't sick. I'd like to be a soldier, too. My mother says the older I get, the more I look like him. My mother says he died of AIDS, so she tries to stop other people getting AIDS.

The house we live in now is smaller than where we used to live. Our old house had running water and electricity, but this house doesn't have anything. After my father died, his family came and took everything we had—our house, our furniture, and our money. My mother is trying to get everything back for us, but she says she needs money to go to court, and we don't have money.

I'm in grade two. My teacher is Mr. Mumba. He's a good teacher. He doesn't yell at us, and says he is proud when we do a good job.

Frank is my best friend. We look out for each other. When I'm late getting to school, he keeps a place for me. Mr. Mumba is a nice teacher but he doesn't like people to be late. My worst subject is arithmetic. I like learning to read and learning about other places in the world.

Of course, what I like to do even better than go to school is play. My friends and I could play with each other all day long and never get tired of it.

Nothing scares me. I'm very brave. I feel bravest when I'm with my friends.

My mother gets scared, though—mostly about money. She sells ribbons on the street in Lusaka. The red ribbons are to remind people about AIDS. The blue ribbons are to remind people not to hit their children. She stops people on the street and asks them to buy a ribbon. Some days she sells a lot of ribbons and brings food home.

There are a lot of children living in this house. They are children whose parents have died, and they have no place to go. I don't know where my mother finds them all, but she does, and she brings them here. She says every child should be taken care of. They are my new brothers and sisters.

MARTHA, 7

I tried to stay very small and secret.

Martha lives in the shed with Collins.

My father died when I was four. He was a nice man. He played games with me and let me sing to him. He had a sickness that made

3

Martha

him very tired, and then he got so tired that he died. The air went out of him, and he was too tired to get it back in again.

My mother has a new husband. He doesn't like me, and would hit me and yell at me. He was angry mostly at night. Agnes says that the dark made him angry, not me. But he yelled at me, not at the dark. At night, I'd be in bed and I'd have to go to the toilet. But I was too scared to go, because if he saw me, he'd hit me. I tried to stay very quiet and very small and secret, but he would still find me and hit me.

I live with Agnes now. It is much nicer. She lets me play, and that makes me happy. A lot of us sleep in one space. I like that. We keep each other warm when it's cold. And it's not so lonely when we're all together. Agnes says it won't be so comfortable when we get bigger, but I don't think we'll get any bigger, so it will be all right. Some of the children are smaller than I am, and some are a little bigger. We are a family now.

My favorite foods are *nsima* (corn porridge) and chicken, although we don't have chicken except as a special treat. When I grow up, I want to be a nurse.

Now that I am with Agnes, the only thing I am afraid of is death. I want to grow to be very, very old.

MANUEL, 8

I wonder.

Manuel lives nearby with his grandmother. She isn't always able to feed him, so he comes to Agnes for many of his meals.

I'm in grade two. The thing I like to do best is practice writing. But I like everything, really.

I live with my grandmother now. My father is in Solwezi. That's far from here, near the Congo. He is there for work. I miss him.

My mother died three months ago. She was sick for a long time. I have two brothers, and we tried to take care of her and make her feel better. But she died anyway. Maybe we should have done a better job. My grandmother says there was nothing my brothers or I could have done because she was going to die anyway. But I wonder.

Sometimes, when my mother wasn't too tired, she'd tell us to clean the house or keep quiet. I liked that, because she was being normal. We'd sing together, too, and she'd put her arm around me and make sure I had something to eat.

Manuel

She died in our house. Her body was there but she wasn't inside it anymore. I went to her funeral. I was very sad, and I get sad all over again when I think of it. A lot of people came. I liked that so many people liked my mother, but they were all over the place. There was nowhere I could go just to be quiet.

Sometimes now, when I am quiet, I can almost feel her. But then I remember that she's dead and I feel sad all over again.

Living with my grandmother isn't bad, although she doesn't have much money and we are hungry a lot. Sometimes Agnes lets me come to her house to eat. I wish my father wasn't so far away.

The thing I am most afraid of is fighting. I never fight, and it scares me to be around people who do. My best friend is Bana. We play together and don't fight with anyone.

VICTOR, 12

I worry that time will pass away.

Victor lives in the neighborhood and helps Agnes with the smaller children.

I live with my mother. My father died a few years ago. I have one sister who is married and is a lot older. My other sister is only a little older than I am.

I don't go to school anymore. I used to go, and I got as far as grade four, but I had to stop because of the death of my father. After he died, I was still able to go to school because my mother could still work. Two years ago, though, she started getting very sick like my father. Now she's too tired to earn money. It was my father's job to send me to school, but he died, so he didn't do his job.

My mother's name is Fostina. She has a boyfriend now. Sometimes he gives her money, and that is how we live. It is a hard life. He doesn't really like me, so I stay out of his way. We can get a bit of food with the money she gets from him, so we can usually eat. There is not enough money for anything extra, like books or pencils.

If my mother's boyfriend decides he doesn't like her anymore, our lives will get harder. She'll have to find a new boyfriend if she's not too tired or sick. Or I could try to get work, carrying things in the market.

Since I don't go to school anymore, I spend my days playing football [soccer] in the alleys. There are a lot of kids around here who are not in school because there's no money in their families. Somebody is sick or somebody has died—dying uses up a lot of money.

Math was my favorite subject in school. It always works. If you know how to do it and you do it properly, math always comes out the way it should. It's clean and makes sense. Some kids didn't like math and made messes of their work, but I liked seeing the numbers all straight in rows. If I ever get to go back to school, I would train to be an accountant because that is all about numbers in straight rows.

My best friend is Luke. He doesn't go to school anymore either. We have other things in common, too. We both have good manners, and neither of us likes to fight. Lots of people think that since we're on the streets a lot, we're rough and always get into trouble. But we're not like that. We talk about how we're going to grow into good people. Sometimes I worry that time will just pass away and I'll never be able to do anything with my life. Luke understands me, and I understand him, and the happiest part of my day is the part I spend with him.

I have heard about AIDS from people who come to our community to teach us. There is a lot about it that I don't know, but I do know that there are a lot of kids like me. They have a mother who is dead or a father who is dead, and their hearts hurt the way mine does.

How will I learn how to be a good man? Luke and I will have to teach each other.

Children of AIDS

...bear witness in favour of those plague-stricken people, so that some memorial of the injustice and outrage done them might endure, and state quite simply what we learn in a time of pestilence: that there are more things to admire in people than to despise.

—ALBERT CAMUS, *French author,* The Plague

Pray for the dead but fight like hell for the living.

—MOTHER JONES, *American labor activist*

BOUNCED AROUND

In Malawi, Mount Mulanje towers over Mulanje Town, a small village that runs along both sides of the two-lane highway. Mud huts and cement-block houses peek through the trees behind the grocery store and gas station.

MITTO, 12

I was hungry all the time.

Mitto lives in a middle-class home with relatives. She has been bounced around between relatives since becoming an orphan.

I would like someone to give me money for a passport, so that I can get away from here.

I am in grade six. English is my best subject. Math is my worst. The thing I like best to do is play football with my friends. My favorite singer is Billy Kawunda, who sings a song I really like, "A Song for Jesus." The house I live in now is nice. It's got a living room with sofas in it and a TV. There is also a dining room, a kitchen, and several bedrooms. We even get satellite TV. Cartoons are what I like best to watch, especially "Scoobie-doo."

I was nine when my father died. He was a good father. He'd take me with him when he went to places—just ordinary places, but I liked to be with him. He'd buy me shoes sometimes. He died of a sickness.

My mother died a year later. They were both sick at the same time, but my father died first. She died of the same thing my father did. My mother really, really, really loved me. She sent me to school, and we would do things together, like wash and dry the dishes.

I'd go to see her a lot when she was in the hospital. I'd feed her porridge because she was too tired to hold the spoon. She used to say, "When I die, you must pray for me." So I do.

When she died, I went to live with my grandmother for a while, but she was old and couldn't look after me, so an aunt in Lilongwe took me in. She wasn't a close aunt, just some sort of relative. This aunt used to hit me and yell at me. She had her own children at the house, but she didn't hit them as much as she hit me. I had to get up earlier than her own children, and do a lot of jobs around the house. If I didn't do things the way she liked, she yelled and hit me.

Every time I ate food at her house, she yelled at me for costing her so much money. She went on and on about how much I ate. I got tired of hearing about it. I would often tell her I wasn't hungry just to stop her yelling. It made me feel so bad. She didn't give me a lunch for school, either. I was hungry all the time. I was able to eat at a friend's house sometimes. That helped.

Also, my brother was there with me. My aunt didn't treat him as badly as she treated me. He used to run away a lot and do odd jobs so he could earn money to buy me food. That helped, too.

After I lived at my aunt's for a while, she started to get sick, too. She was coughing and coughing. It was scary for me because I'd seen it before with my parents. She died at her house.

I was moved again. Now I live in Mulanje with another relative.

My favorite clothes are trousers, especially pedal-pushers. I have a blue pair and a black pair. I help out here by clearing the table, washing

CHILD LABOR

The International Labor Organization estimates that there are 246 million children around the world who have jobs that keep them out of school most or all of the time. Children do backbreaking labor as brick-makers, on farms, in factories, and in brothels. Ten million of them, mostly girls, work as domestic servants—virtually as slaves. When children are considered too old to work, or get old enough to start demanding to be paid, they are tossed aside without protection, without money, and far from their families.

Extreme poverty forces many parents to send their children to work to help keep the family from starving. Parents may also hope that having their child learn a trade at an early age is the best hope for them in the long run. The benefits of a school education seem a long way off when the family is hungry now. Many countries also charge fees for school, supplies, and uniforms, which poor families are unable to pay.

Children who don't have parents to look out for them are the most vulnerable to exploitation by employers. The rising number of AIDS orphans means there is an ever-increasing pool of children to be drawn on, used up, and tossed away.

In Malawi, children work on the big tea and tobacco plantations, built during Colonial times. In addition to missing school, they face dangers from chemicals, cutting tools, snake and insect bites, and heavy workloads. Nearly half of Malawi's children between the ages of 10 and 14 are laborers.

dishes, and looking after myself so I don't make more work for others. No one hits me here, and I'd like to keep it that way.

I pray so I can make myself happy. I'm happy when I'm at school. Mr. Moses is my teacher. He is a very good teacher. He doesn't hit us, and if we don't understand something, we can ask questions. He also gives us food.

I get afraid when I dream about snakes, or when I dream that my mother, father, and aunt want me to join them being dead.

I have malaria now. I've had it before. A mosquito bit me. A mosquito can make you very sick. My body feels like someone hit me all over with a big stick. I have pain everywhere, a headache, a bad stomach, and I'm cold and hot. I'm taking medicine but I still feel bad.

I like to read English stories—any kind of English stories. And I like to play with toys. I also help out at the local nursery school, teaching the little kids. When there's a football game at my school, I lead the cheers. We sing and dance around the football field. People spend more time watching us than they do watching the game.

Living here is fine, but there's a lot of yelling. Sometimes the yelling is at me, and sometimes there's just general yelling. The thing I want most is a passport. There must be happier places.

Although the world is full of suffering,
it is also full of the overcoming of it.

—HELEN KELLER, *Deaf and Blind*
American author and educator

NEW DESKS

Lukata, a village an hour outside of Lusaka in Zambia, is not even on a map. It's way off the highway, through scrub brush and grassy fields, down sandy roads that aren't really roads.

I am traveling today with some people from an organization called Children In Crisis (CIC). We drive past small, round mud homes with thatched grass roofs and tiny patches of straight-rowed gardens.

On the way to the village, we see two small boys clearing the land with machetes, getting it ready for planting. A CIC worker talks to the adult in charge of them and gets permission for the boys to come with us to the school. They jump into the truck with us. We gather several more children along the way.

The school is in a clearing. There is great excitement today. The desks have arrived.

Children celebrating the arrival of their new desks

MAVIS, 15

I'm still alive.

I live with my grandmother and my brothers and sisters. Some cousins live with us, too. There's not really room enough for all of us in my grandmother's small house, but we manage.

Both of my parents are dead. They died when I was younger. They were sick, which is why they died. Whenever I get sick, I worry that I will die, too. But so far, I'm still alive.

For a long time my village didn't have a school. Then everyone got together and built one. We made the mounds for the bricks, gathered the mud, and baked the bricks. I was too young to do much, but I did what I could. Everyone did. I saw the pile of bricks grow and grow until finally there was enough. They built one building for the school and one building to be a home for the teachers. Later they built more classrooms. People in the village sewed our uniforms, too.

They were able to make desks for the grade seven class. This is the most serious class. Students in grade seven have to take the exam that will tell them if they qualify to go on to secondary school, so they have to study hard.

Up until today everyone else had to sit on rocks in the yard, or on the floor of the classroom. As of today, everyone has desks. Money came from UNICEF, and now a group called Children in Crisis has brought us all these desks.

Even though most of us don't have shoes, we have uniforms, and we now have desks. This shows we are all serious students.

English is my best subject. Science is the worst, but it isn't too bad. We have a lot of things to do at this school. I don't know what it's like at other schools in the world, but at this school, we all work to keep it looking nice. We work in the flower gardens, we keep the stones lined up straight along the pathways, and we sweep the dirt in the yard with branches so it looks good. We sweep out the classrooms, too, of course. This is *our* school, and we want it to be as good a place as we can make it. We even take turns cleaning out the lavatories!

I think I'll be a nurse when I finish school. There will always be sick people, so I'll always have a job. A lot of people have AIDS, and it makes them get sick a lot. It would be a lot of hard work, but I'm used to doing hard work. I work at home, too. I have to cook, get water, sweep, clean, and wash dishes. There is always work to do. You can never say, "Well, I'm done, there's no more work." There's always more work.

At least when I'm a nurse, when my workday is over, I'll be done for that day. I don't think I'll have a boyfriend, because he will probably mean more work. It would be nice for a while, but the nice part wouldn't last. I've seen how it is with other girls.

MARY, 13

Someone thinks I'm important.

I live with my grandmother and with my mother. My father died last spring. I don't know why he died, except that he was sick.

I am the second child in my family. I have two brothers and sisters. Science and math are my best subjects. I'd like to be a teacher when I grow up.

I'm so happy to have a desk! All my life I have sat on the floor of the schoolroom, or on a rock in the schoolyard. It is uncomfortable, and it is hard to write that way, although my mind is smart and I still learn. I know I will be a better student now. Having a desk makes me feel important. Having a desk makes me feel that someone else thinks I'm important.

We hear about AIDS, and there are a lot of children in this village who live with their grandmother or their aunt, but no one says why. People die. We hear about that all the time—that there is a funeral for this person or that person.

I don't have a boyfriend. I don't want one. I want to play net ball with my friends, and sing, and study at my new desk. If there is a boy who will make me happy and still let me do all the things I want to do, then maybe I'll have a boyfriend.

I have another wish. I have never been to Lusaka. I hear that it is an exciting place. Maybe someday I'll get to see it.

OSCAR, 17

I am afraid of losing me.

My mother is dead. I live with my father. He is part of the Parent Teacher Association here. He is helping to put together the desks today. He also works in the school garden to grow things for us to eat.

Math is my best subject. Science is my worst. I am the oldest child in my family. I have six brothers and three sisters. I know I look younger than I am. I have sickle-cell anemia. It has made me smaller than I should be, and has turned a patch of my hair white. My red blood cells are supposed to look like circles, but they look like sickles instead. It makes me tired, and I get sick a lot. Still, it's important for me to look after my brothers and sisters, since that is my job, as the oldest.

My mother died a year ago. I think about her all the time. She was sick for a while. We all helped to take care of her. I miss her a lot. We all do.

Singing makes me feel better, especially church songs. I'm in the choir at school. People tell me I have a good voice, and I think they are right, although I don't think I'll be able to do it for money. What I would like to do for money is be a bus driver so I could go to other places.

Death is the only thing that scares me. Many people here, including lots of children, have had someone die on them. My mother was with us. Now she's gone. I am afraid of losing other people I love, and I am afraid of losing me.

ORPHANS

- Around the world, there are now 15 million AIDS orphans, 11.5 million in Sub-Saharan Africa.

- By 2020, there will be 20 million AIDS orphans in Sub-Saharan Africa.

- Over 30 million children in Africa are orphans from other causes (e.g., war).

- Asia has over 87 million orphans, from all causes. The number of AIDS orphans is still small but growing.

- In Ethiopia in 2002, more than 75% of the domestic workers were orphans, many working 11 hours a day, 7 days a week, often unpaid, unable to go to school.

- In Zambia in 2002, the average age of children working as prostitutes was 15. Almost 75% of these children were orphans.

- Orphans don't get enough food; therefore they are more likely to be smaller than non-orphans of the same age.

- Orphans are less likely to be able to stay in school.

Does the road wind up hill all the way?
Yes, to the very end.
Will the day's journey take the whole long day?
From morn to night, my friend.

—CHRISTINA ROSSETTI, *English poet*

THE ISLAND IN THE SKY

Mount Mulanje, in Malawi, is known as the Island in the Sky because of the way the mist appears to cut off the mountain along the middle, making the peak look like it is floating in air. It is a mountain of deep green, from the tea estates that surround it and from the pine forest that climbs up its rocky sides.

The organization called Friends of Mulanje Orphans has invited me to one of their feeding centers. With money raised in England, members of the community can come together to provide the many orphans in the area with one meal a day.

The pickup truck we are driving only starts when everyone gathers around to give it a push. We drive down bumpy, narrow roads that are little more than red dirt pathways. The homes are round mud huts with thatched grass rooftops. Chickens squawk and dash out of our way. In some yards, people work in small vegetable plots or rest on small benches outside the huts.

We arrive at the feeding station, a brick building in a clearing. A girl pounds maize with a large stick. Grandmothers stoke the fires under huge pots of nsima and beans.

Children start arriving. The shed quickly fills up, but still more children come, running down pathways from all directions. The clearing is soon full. The children are excited. They're hungry, and they're about to eat.

The rooms of the shed are barren of furniture, except for a few benches. Along the walls, in neat rows, are broad, shallow bowls of nsima and beans. The children spread straw mats on the floor to sit on.

The older ones look after the younger ones. Hands must be washed, since food is eaten with their fingers. They sing me a welcome song and then sing grace, giving thanks for the food.

The clearing is quiet as the children eat. After the meal, they wash their plates, sing some more songs, and some of them tell me their stories.

LONI, 13

I felt like the world had stopped.

I come from Nkhonya Village, across the bridge. I am in seventh grade. My best subject is English. Science is my worst. When I can play with my friends, I like to play games like net ball and skipping. I live with my three brothers. My grandmother takes care of all of us.

Both of my parents are dead. No one explained what was wrong with them. They just got sick, and then they died.

I was five when my mother died. She died in the hospital. After she died, my father went away to another village and left us kids with my grandmother. But he would come back now and then, and give my grandmother some money. I was always glad to see him, and he was always glad to see me.

Then he got sick and he came back to us for good. He stayed in another house in the village because there wasn't room for him at Gogo's (Grandmother's). I would go to see him every day—to see if there was anything he needed. Sometimes he seemed to get a little better, but then he would just get sick again.

That was my life for a while. I went to school, went to see my father, and went back to my grandmother's. Then one day at school, I got a message that I was not to go to my father's house. My father had died. I felt like the world had stopped.

Other things went on as before—school, living with Gogo—but everything was different, too. Our problems got bigger. My father didn't help us much when he was sick, but we kept thinking he would get better. Gogo spent her money on medicines for him, thinking he would get better and be able to take care of us. But he died, and we had no money. Gogo spent her savings trying to make him better, and then burying him.

I had to leave school and do lots of work to help Gogo. I looked after the house and the other kids while she tried to earn money. We still didn't have enough food, though.

Someone told us about this feeding center, so now my brothers and I come every day. We are only allowed to come if we are in school, so I can go to classes again. Now it doesn't matter so much if my grandmother has no money because my brothers and I eat here at the Orphan Club.

I like the activities here, especially the singing. I am one of the singing leaders. I like that. If I can lead people in singing, maybe I can lead them in other things, too. I go to church as well, and sing in the choir. I am happiest when I sing. Singing makes me feel like I can do anything.

In Gogo's house, we all sleep in one room, on the floor. We put straw mats down. We are short of blankets, and have to share. One day, I would like to have my own blanket.

The only thing that makes me afraid is AIDS. It can kill you, and there is no medicine. Maybe that's what killed my parents. I don't know. No one told me.

I would like to be a nun when I grow up. I have always wanted this. When I am a nun I will always be clean, and I will be around people I can look after and who will look after me. I will spend my days praying to God and singing.

ANGELLA, 12

I live in heaven.

I live with my Gogo, me and my brother and sister. I am the middle child. My favorite things to do are singing and net ball. I also like being with my friends. We like to act out plays together, sometimes for other people, and sometimes just for ourselves.

My village is called Kumwamba. It means heaven. I like to tell people that I live in heaven.

I was six years old when my mother died. She kept getting bad headaches. We had to be very quiet when we played so our voices wouldn't hurt her head. She stayed at the house while she was sick. Gogo looked after her. She got thinner and thinner. She hardly looked like my mother anymore.

I don't really remember when my mom died. I was very small. My father died when I was four, so I remember even less about that. I remember things about them, though, like the way my father laughed and swung me up into the air, so that my head was in the trees. I remember my mother putting a dress on me and telling me to try to stay clean for a little while.

My mother looked after my father, and then he died. My Gogo looked after my mother, and then my mother died. I get scared when I get sick, in case I might die, too.

Here is my usual day: I get up when the sky starts to get light. I wash the dishes from the night before, because it's dark when we finish eating in the evening. Then I heat up more water so I can wash myself. I wash, get dressed, and go to school.

English is the subject I like best. Science is the worst. It's only things to memorize, and I don't like it. After school, I come to the Orphan Club, eat, do things with other kids, then I go home again.

If there is any food at home, I eat again, but there usually isn't, so I don't. If there's extra money to buy paraffin for the lamp, then I read, but there usually isn't, so I just go to bed when it's too dark to do anything else. The only thing I have to read is my school textbook for social studies. It's mostly about natural disasters. I've read it a lot. I know all about natural disasters.

There are two things that make me happy—coming to the Orphan Club and getting home before dark so that Gogo won't yell at me. There are only two things that make me afraid. One is AIDS, which can't be seen. The other is a snake, which can be seen. I've seen some big snakes. I don't like those.

When I finish school, I want to be a nurse so that I can do something about all these sick people.

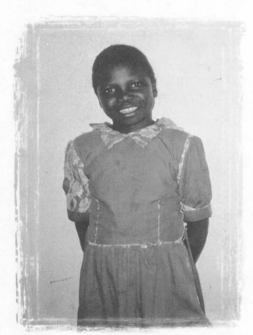

MODESTA, 12

I'm a very good cook.

I'm in grade four. At school, I like sports best. I guess we have to learn other things, but I'd rather play sports all the time.

I live with my grandmother and my two younger sisters. Being the oldest, I have to do more work than they do. As soon as I get up, I have to wash the pots and pans we used for supper the night before—if we had food. It's too dark to wash them by the time we finish eating. One day I'd like them to magically wash themselves at night so that I don't have to do it.

In the house there are two children older than I am—cousins, I guess. They're boys so they don't do anything. I don't like them. They swear a lot. They were living with my grandmother before we came along. Their parents are dead, too, but that hasn't made them any nicer.

I was nine when my mother died. She died in our home, but she was sick for a long time before she died. I used to look after her. She had terrible headaches, and she was very weak and thin. I'd fetch her water and help her wash. I'd wash her back for her. Sometimes she had a bad rash on her body and in her mouth. She hurt all over, even when she ate. I'd do all the housework, too, so she wouldn't have to worry about it. I even made my little sisters behave. I'd cook for her, too, and try to make her eat so she'd get strong again. I'd cook nsima, like she showed me. I'm a very good cook.

As soon as my mother died, my father disappeared. I don't know where he went. I haven't seen him since she died. I don't think he's coming back. Lots of fathers don't.

Life was easier when my mother was alive. I know she loved me. She took care of us. She made sure we ate and had clothes. She made sure we didn't talk back. There's really no one to do that now. Our grandmother is too tired.

My mother made Christmas special. We'd sing and make decorations out of things we'd find around. It was a happy time. Now it's nothing. Now it's just a day.

DALITSO, 13

I thought I would die.

I have five brothers and six sisters. I live in Mandanda village, three kilometers from here. Both of our parents are dead. My oldest sister takes care of us. She's nice, and not too often in a bad mood. She also has a volunteer job, teaching some of the adults in the village how to read.

I have chores to do at home. We all do. How would we manage if we didn't? I work in the garden at home, growing vegetables. I also have to sweep the yard and keep it looking tidy. I don't mind doing it. It's my job, so it's up to me to be sure to do it properly.

My mother died in the hospital. She had TB, and she had other things wrong with her before that. She kept getting sick. I would go to visit her there. She told us to do well in school and take care of each other. I think she knew she was going to die. She was very sad.

My father died when I was much younger. I don't know what was wrong with him. He coughed a lot, and was very tired. He used to play with us. He and I would sometimes hold hands and chase the chickens around the yard.

I used to be in a wheelchair. Two years ago, I couldn't walk.

My mother died two years ago. After her funeral, I had diarrhea for three days. I was in bed during that time. One day, when I tried to get up, I couldn't move my right leg. For a week or so, I used a big stick to help me get around. At the end of that week, my left leg became paralyzed, too. The stick didn't help me after that.

I was sent down to the Queen Elizabeth Hospital in Blantyre. The doctors looked at me, but they couldn't discover why my legs stopped working.

It was awful, being in the hospital. People kept dying around me. I thought I would die, too, and they would just haul my body away and give my bed to someone else, like I was no more than a bag of maize to be put out of the way. But I didn't die.

A year ago, I started walking again. For three days I had vomiting and diarrhea. The day after that, the feeling started coming back into my legs. First I could feel my toes, then I could move my feet. I stood up against a wall and, bit by bit, started to walk again. At first, all I could do was move slowly.

Now I can dance.

I want to be a doctor when I grow up. I remember how it was with me, so I want to help.

ERUBY, 13

We were taken to the wrong funeral.

I have two sisters. I used to have a little brother, but he died when he was just a toddler. I don't know why he died.

The things I like best are playing net ball and singing. I like writing and memorizing poems, too.

My mother died when I was nine. She was in the hospital for a while, but then she came home. She died at home. I didn't know what happened at first. I was on the veranda, looking at all these people who were crying in the yard. Then someone told me and I cried, too.

My father died a year later. He was sick for a long time at home, and then he went to the hospital to die. He spent a lot of time in bed before he died, just like my mother.

No one took my sisters and me to his funeral. There were two funerals on the same day. My uncle died at almost the same time as my father. There was a mix-up, and we were taken to the wrong funeral. We were at my uncle's funeral, and we missed our father's.

Gogo looks after us now.

Mother used to *really* look after us. She made sure we were all right—that we ate and had clothes and didn't fight with each other. Gogo can't do all that. She's too old.

Gogo doesn't have a real job. She has to make her own job. She looks for wood in the bushes, gathers it together, and sells it. My older sister helps her sell the wood. I help her look for it. I also wash dishes and clothes for her and help around the house. It's just us now. We have to look out for each other.

In my future, I see myself as a nurse. To get there, I will keep on with school.

Singing and dancing make me happiest. When I sing and dance, I forget my problems.

What am I afraid of? I'm not afraid of anything!

Children performing an anti-AIDS play

Africa after AIDS will be an unpredictable place. What will
happen to the minds of a generation that grows up alone, poor, and
ashamed by the stigma of the disease that killed their parents?
… A whole generation is carrying a millstone of sadness.

—EMMA GUEST, *Author of* Children of AIDS

ON THE STREET

The Chisomo Youth Center in Blantyre, Malawi, sits on a hill over-looking a valley full of closely built homes, secondhand clothing stalls, and coffin shops. The boys who find their way here have been living on the streets, trying to make a life for themselves that is better than the one they left behind. Most are orphans. As AIDS kills off more parents, the number of street children will continue to grow.

Most street children are boys. They don't last long in this rough life, but they last longer than girls, who generally end up as prostitutes or domestic slaves.

CHIPEERO, 17

I ate anything.

I was born in the western part of Zomba region, in the mountains. My mother and father are still alive. They are sick a lot but they are still alive. My mother is a businesswoman. She sells secondhand shoes from a blanket by the side of the road. My father sells bananas, but not on the same street where my mother sells shoes. He moves around with his bananas.

I am living with my parents again, after being on the street for a while. We are living in a region of Blantyre, outside the main part of

the city. It is not a very nice place, but it is somewhere to be.

I have had a lot of troubles. There are many children in my family, and my father is a poor man. There was never enough food, even before my parents started getting sick. When they are sick, there is even less money because they can't work, and we spend money on medicine.

My father said I talked back too much. He said it added to his burden, and he beat me, so I ran away.

I left home to live on the streets in 1998, when I was 12. I came to Blantyre, a big city, because I thought that here I could get money and have food to eat and a better life.

Life was not better. My father was not there to beat me, but other people were. There were many hostile things in the city, lots of trouble. It was hard to find work.

Sometimes I would get money by helping people carry things. Sometimes I would carry things for people, and afterwards, they would refuse to pay me.

If I got a little money, I could buy a little food—bananas, nsima—I ate anything.

There are many things to be afraid of in the city. If I earned money, one of the larger boys on the street would often steal it from me, beating me to get it. Who could I go to? I could not go to the police.

Sometimes the police would gather up all the street boys they could and take them to Maula Prison, the boys' prison. Sometimes the boys they take have stolen things, or have gone with other men for money. Men will sometimes make boys do things with their bodies, and then give them a bit of money afterwards. Sometimes the police just don't like the look of the boys.

AIDS is a killer disease. Many of the boys I knew on the street had no parents, because AIDS had taken them away. They were just children, many of them smaller than I am, and they were living on the street because their parents were dead, and no one would care for them.

On the street, I have seen boys who are very sick. Maybe they had AIDS; maybe they had something else. It is hard to be on the street, and even harder if you are sick. There is no comfort anywhere.

I will always keep myself safe from AIDS. I am a man, and I will look after myself, as a man should.

It was hard for me to go back to my family, but the Center helped me. One of their people saw me on the street and invited me to come here for a meal. They treated me well and talked to me like they cared, so I kept coming back. Now they pay my school fees and buy me school supplies, so I'm back at school and studying. I'm going to make something of myself. My best subjects are agriculture, geography, and biology.

I think I would like to be a lawyer, because lawyers make a lot of money. I'll give my family a lot of money, then do all I can to help other boys who live on the street.

FAMPHATSO, 16

I slept anywhere.

I was born in the Chor district around Blantyre. Now I live in Glad Township. I live with my mother, three sisters, and two brothers. I'm the oldest, which is a lot of responsibility.

My father died a lot of years ago. I don't know what he died of. My mother knows, but she won't tell me.

My mother is sick now. She has TB. She got it from going to the bars and drinking beer. She got money from doing that, too, but not a lot of money. She is very sick. Sometimes she gets a little bit better, and then she gets very sick again. She's been like this for two years. She coughs a lot and she is very weak. I hate to see her like this. She is very beautiful, but the sickness makes her feel not beautiful.

I do piece work [work paid according to the amount produced instead of by the hour], odd jobs now and then to help her out with a bit of money. Sometimes we can pay for medicine and she gets a bit better, but she never stays well. She says I should stop buying the medicine because it doesn't really do any good. We don't have the money for it now anyway.

Not all of us live at home anymore, just my brother and me. The others are in a children's home. Sometimes I go there to visit them, but not very often. I don't have time usually. I'm always trying to earn money.

When I was 12, I left home to live on the streets. There was no food at home. Even before my mother got sick, we were always hungry. I am the oldest child. It was my responsibility to earn money. I begged, mostly, because there wasn't much work for me since I was so small. If I managed to get a little extra money, I'd take it home to my mother, but there usually wasn't anything extra. Other boys, bigger ones, would beat me and steal my money.

I learned which foods were cheap and filled my stomach fast. I slept anywhere—by the side of the road, where the buses come and go, in the bushes. When it rained, I got wet. I shivered a lot because I had no blanket.

I was sick with malaria once and went into the hospital. It was a horrible place. They put me into a bed with a stranger who smelled bad. I didn't know who he was, but they made me share a single bed with him because there were no other beds. A lot of people died while I was there. A lot of people were sick with TB or AIDS. I was afraid of catching something from them. I was scared and lonely and unhappy.

When I was living on the streets in Blantyre, a friend told me about the Chisomo Youth Center. I came, they fed me, and they let me stay here to get some rest. They helped me go home. The younger ones in my family are too much for my mother to handle now that she is so sick, so they are staying elsewhere.

I go to school now in the morning. Then I go to a training place to learn to be a haircutter. I try to earn money, too, and sometimes I even find time for a game of football!

I don't want to be a haircutter all my life, though. One day I would like to start my own organization to help street kids. There are so many of us. We learned today about human rights. Even children have the right to have a good life, with food and school and things like that. We had a good discussion about that today, and we had some food. Today I feel good.

KINSLEY, 14

You have to be very strong.

There are eight children in my family. I am the sixth. My father is dead. My mother lives in a village in Dedza, with some of the other children. I live with my brother, in a village near Dilante.

I was very young when my father died. My mother works as a farmer, growing maize. She sells what she grows after the harvest. She does not have much land, so there is not much to sell. When she gets sick, she can't work, and then there was no food.

I went to live with my brother because there was not enough food in my mother's house. My brother's wife, my sister-in-law, treated me very badly. She gave me a lot of work to do—work that hurts me. For example, she would send me to the ADMARC [food warehouse store] to buy a bag of maize. I would have to carry this bag home on my back. It was very heavy, and I'd have to move very slowly as I carried it. She'd send me out early, without any food. When I got back, all the food she had prepared for the family would be eaten, so I'd get no food that day.

I left them after a while. I was getting no more to eat there than I did with my mother, so why would I stay?

I went to live on the street. You have to be very strong, or you'll never manage to do it. You are often cold, often hungry, often scared. Sometimes, when it rained, I would be wet and cold at the same time. My body would ache from shaking and from my teeth chattering. There was no way to get warm. The nights were very long, then, because the cold and wet would not let me escape into sleep.

Another bad thing that would happen is that money would be stolen from me. The bigger guys on the street watch to see who is working. When I got paid, they'd beat me up and steal my money. I always tried to buy something to eat as soon as I could after being paid, so at least I'd have something in my belly after the day's work. But it didn't always happen that way.

I'd see people doing evil things to each other on the street, things I don't want to talk about.

I'd sleep on pieces of cardboard when I could find them. They were softer than just sleeping right on the ground. I might find the cardboard, and then hide it in the morning. But it was almost always gone again when I went to find it at night.

There were some good times, too. I met some other boys on the street, boys like me, and we would hang out together and take care of each other. Sometimes we'd beg. Once, someone gave me 200 *kwatcha* [$2.00 US]. It was fun to have so much money.

But friends you make on the street don't last long. Someone is always getting beat up, or sick, or picked up by the police, or is offered money by a man and is taken away and never seen again. You can't rely a whole lot on friends you make on the street. It's a day-by-day thing.

After I was living on the street for a while, a friend named Mike told me about Chisomo. I came here and they let me sleep here for a few days. It was wonderful to have a safe place to spend the night. They let me get rested up while they contacted my brother.

I'm back living with my brother and his wife. Chisomo talked to them, and they treat me better now. It helps that I can come here sometimes to eat. I don't feel like such a burden on them, and my brother's wife isn't so mean anymore.

Being hungry is a terrible thing. It makes you feel like you have no worth, like you have no power. When I finish school, I would like to be a soldier or a musician—whichever would give me food regularly. I don't ever want to be hungry again.

YAMIKANI, 13

It was dangerous to have money.

My father is dead. I don't know exactly when he died. It was a little while ago. He died of some illness. I don't know what illness. No one told me. My mother lives in Dilante. She is sick, too. I am an only child.

My mother stays at home when she can't find work. When she works, it is just now and then, very short jobs, like cleaning a rich person's house, or doing their laundry, or maybe selling something.

There was no food at home, and I got tired of being hungry, so I decided to go live on the streets. When I was at home my mother worried more, because she couldn't feed me. Sometimes, when there was just a little bit of food in the house, she'd give it to me and she'd stay hungry. I got tired of watching that happen.

When I was on the street, I used to beg from white people because they always have lots of money. Some white people ride around in cars. Some walk around with big bundles on their backs. It doesn't matter. They all have money.

Some white people would give me money. Some would walk right by me as if I wasn't talking to them.

Sometimes I'd do car watching. Watching cars goes like this: someone pays you to watch their car for them, to make sure that no one, like other street kids, damages it.

It was bad not to have money. But it was also dangerous to have money, because if the older kids knew I had money, they'd beat me up and take it. Sometimes adults would beat me up and take the money, too, if they knew I had any. You couldn't trust anyone. When I had money I could hold onto, I'd buy food.

I slept on top of a sack when it was hot. When it was cold, I wrapped the sack around me like a blanket.

I met the director of Chisomo on the street one day. He told me what Chisomo does and where it is, and said I should come here. So I did. I've been coming here for a few months now.

I'm back with my mother. I walk here every day from Dilante, which is about five kilometers away. I still beg and do things like watching cars for money. It's easier on my mother that I come to Chisomo, because I get food here. On days I don't come here, I usually don't eat. My mother and I live in a small house with two little rooms, surrounded by other small houses.

Of course, I know about AIDS. It's a disease that has no medicine. It will kill you. I'm not going to get it, I've decided. I'm going to grow up to be a mechanic.

HARRIS, 14

When she walked, it looked like sticks moving.

I know a lot about AIDS. You can get it if you share a razor blade with someone, if their blood touches your blood. It makes you lose a lot of weight and then you die.

There are four children in my family. I am

the third. My mother and father are dead. They were both sick, but my father didn't die from sickness. He died because he was in a car accident. The people around the accident took him out of his car and beat him, and he died from that.

My mother died from TB. She died in her home village. When she got sick, she lost her good color. She used to be sort of plump, but she lost all her weight. When she walked, it looked like sticks moving.

I took care of her as long as I could, but I couldn't do everything. It got too hard for me, so I told her she should go to her home village. I stayed there with her until she died. There were other people helping me take care of her, so it wasn't so hard for me.

After she died, I stayed with my mother's younger sister. She loved me very well, as if she were my own mother.

She could not take care of all of us, though. When my younger brother went to stay with her, I came back to the city. I wasn't really used to village life anyway. I've always lived in the city, and the village is very different.

In the city, I stayed with my two older brothers, but they were both in school and didn't have a lot of money to spare. They could not really look after me, although they let me stay with them. Sometimes my oldest brother would break rocks in a quarry for a day or two, and get money so he could buy food. But it was never very much.

Sometimes I would try to find jobs, like watching cars or carrying things in the market. I'd buy food so my brothers wouldn't have to feed me.

When I finish school, I want to be an actor. I've been in a lot of plays, at Chisomo and at school. I really enjoy it, and this is what I'd like to spend my life doing.

- 10 million children in Africa live on the streets.
- In Brazzaville, Congo, and in Lusaka, Zambia, over half of all street children are AIDS orphans.
- Children living on the street often have to commit crimes (like stealing) in order to survive. A 1991 study in Brazil showed that over 80% of the prison inmates were former street children.
- The number of street children in Blantyre, Malawi, increased 150% in 2000; 80% of these street children were AIDS orphans.
- The International Labor Organization has discovered that 85% of the child prostitutes in Zambia have never been to school; a growing number are AIDS orphans.

TROUBLE

All that we know who land in jail
Is that the wall is strong;
And that each day is like a year,
A year whose days are long.

—Oscar Wilde,
Irish novelist, playwright, and poet

In any country, prisoners get very little financial aid. In a country that has been made poorer by AIDS, people in prison have even less than usual.

I wanted to see for myself how AIDS has impacted the lives of young people in trouble. To do this, I visited two prisons for boys in Malawi. I've visited kids in prison in other countries, too. The hardest part is walking away and leaving them there.

Richimani and Mateni are in the Mpemba Boys Home, outside Blantyre. The Home is a series of small buildings in a large grassy area surrounded by trees. Some of the buildings are dormitories. Each boy has a bed to himself, with a small cupboard beside it. All the boys come from very poor families. Only half of them have shoes.

RICHIMANI, 16

There was nothing soft or easy.

My father is dead. I used to live with my mother, but I left because there was nothing to eat.

I got to grade two in school. My best subjects were math and religious education.

My father was ill for a long time. He was often too weak and tired to work. After he died we had nothing. Anything we had before, we spent on medicines for my father, but they didn't help him. Then there was the cost of his funeral. My mother remarried but we still had nothing. I didn't even have enough clothes to keep warm. I had an empty stomach but nothing else.

I stole to look after myself. I stole food and little things that I could sell to get food. Once I stole twenty kwatcha from my mother so I could get something to eat.

I am in here for stealing a Panasonic radio. It was in someone else's house. The radio was by an open window, and I reached in and took it. I was going to sell it, but I was arrested before I could do that. The police came to arrest me at five in the morning. Everything was still dark. They tied my hands behind my back, and took me away.

I was very scared.

First they took me to the community police depot. Then they took me to the Choro police station. I was held there for two months. It was horrible to be in that cell for two months. I was in there with men much older than me. They didn't beat me, but they made fun of me when I looked scared. And they would try to make me more scared.

The cell was just a cement room with a toilet. There was nothing soft or easy about it. I was afraid I would never get out. I never saw a lawyer. No one saw a lawyer.

Then I was brought to the Mpemba Boys Home. This is not a bad place. I sleep in a real bed instead of on cement, and there is food for me to eat. I can also go to school and they teach us a trade. Sometimes we play football. My life is better here than it has been in a long time.

I will be here for two years more. When I get out, I would eventually like to be a typist in an office. That would be easy work. I would wear clean clothes every day and be paid every week.

This place is far from where my mother lives, and it is difficult for her to come to see me. She also has other worries. Her health is not good and she still has no money. I hope she does not die before I get out. I try not to think about how much I miss her. I try to think about how lucky I am instead.

MATENI, 16

Was it right?

I come from a family of five brothers. None of them come to see me. They don't know I am here. My mother and father are dead, of a long illness. They got sicker and sicker, and thinner and thinner, until they got too sick to get better again.

I lived with my brothers until May 2002. A man came to my home and asked me to go to work for him in another town, selling groceries along the road. I needed money—I was hungry—so I went away with him. I was 14.

I worked for him for three months, but he never paid me. He just gave me a bit of nsima every day, sometimes with beans, but usually without. I got tired of being mistreated. I gathered up all his goods that I was supposed to be selling for him, and I sold them for myself, keeping the money. I went to another village, hoping he wouldn't find me.

He found me. He brought the police with him, and they arrested me. The police went through my pockets. They took all the money I had on me and gave it to my employer. I tried to tell them that I had worked for him for three months without being paid. But they did not want to hear about that. Nothing happened to the man who cheated me.

They took me to the police station and put me in a cell. I was there for two days, and then I was brought here. I have to be here for another two years and seven months.

We are kept busy here all day long. It's not a bad life. At least we eat, and we can learn things.

We get up early, clean our barracks, have breakfast, go to classes, have lunch, and then do vocational training, like carpentry or bricklaying. After that, on most days, we can have a football game. There's a junior football field and a senior football field. We go to sleep in the evenings. We don't have much free time. At Christmas some people came and gave us gifts, like fruit drinks, biscuits, and soap.

I was 13 when my parents died. I miss them. One of my brothers died, too, of the same illness. I wonder sometimes if they are together in heaven, if they know I'm here. I hope they will be proud of me one day.

The thing that scares me the most is when I think that my other brothers might die while I'm in here.

I guess what I did was wrong, but was it right for that man to cheat me? A lot of things are not right. But things could be worse.

When I get out of here, I would like to be a driver of some kind—a taxi driver, or minibus driver, or a truck driver. I don't know how to drive yet, but I can learn. A lot of people do it. How hard can it be?

- One million African children have had a teacher die of AIDS.

- In the first 10 months of 1998, Zambia lost 1300 teachers to AIDS.

- A study done in Congo of AIDS orphans showed that many have psycho-social problems such as post-traumatic stress, which shows up by kids running away from home. Their problems include being disruptive in school; displaying aggressive behavior and elective mutism (refusing to talk); suffering depression and anxiety; and feeling unwanted and like a failure.

- Orphaned children have less hope that their futures will be good. They expect that they will die soon, and that they will not have a chance to be happy.

- Orphans in Zambia say they no longer feel loved and don't think they have a part to play in society.

- Orphans separated from their brothers and sisters feel even more isolated.

- Orphans are less likely to stay in school.

A coffin-maker's workshop

PRISON

There are some who speculate that the current violence in Zimbabwe and Congo may have been sparked by the feeling of hopelessness affecting a generation who know they do not have long to live.... If you expect to die within a decade, you have little to lose from trying to violently seize the property of those richer than you.

—EMMA GUEST, *English author,*
Children of AIDS

Maula Prison Farm, outside Lilongwe, is clearly a prison. It is set back among fields of maize and long grass. The prisoners wear white uniforms and bend over crops. On the other side of the road from the prison is a row of shacks belonging to the guards and their families. High fences with barbed wire surround everything. Visitors have to pass through a gate. The food parcels they bring for family members are checked over.

Most of the prisoners here are adult males. Those in white uniforms have already been sentenced. The prison also has a building for women and one for young boys. I am told that most of the women are in for murdering their male partners or for killing their babies when they are unable to feed them.

I am taken through two sets of fences to the welfare office, a shack that sits inside its own fenced-in yard. The welfare officer apologizes for the cramped conditions. There is almost nowhere to sit. The Youth Watch Society has set up a small industry in the prison, where some of the boys can make soap for themselves and the other prisoners. The supplies are stored in the welfare office.

While I'm waiting for the boys to be called down, I go out into the yard. The tin building that houses the women is on a little hill behind us. Many women are outside, airing clothes and talking. I wave. They smile and wave back.

The guards bring in three boys. They bow low to the adults as they enter the hut. They sit on up-turned buckets and tell me about their lives.

FRANCIS, 17

I want a quiet life.

I come from Lukuni. I got as far as the seventh grade.

I have been here for seven months. I was in court once but nothing happened. I was supposed to go today, but that didn't happen. I don't know when my trial will be. I was arrested for burglary eight months ago.

Both of my parents are dead. My mother died when I was 8, my father when I was 13. Both died from a long sickness. They coughed and got very thin. I dropped out of school a year or two after my mother died. There just didn't seem to be any point in going. I missed her and my heart hurt all the time. It got in the way of thinking. Plus, there never was any money in the family. I was already working when my father died. I did odd jobs. For a while I cut up potatoes for the chip fryers on the street.

There was a burglary at a shop in Seegwa. My friend Steve and I were nearby when it happened, but we didn't do the stealing. Some people saw us nearby. Steve and I went down to the river to do our laundry. The man from the shop followed us down there, and then fetched the police. They said if we weren't the ones to rob the shop, we should take them to the ones who did. I said we were innocent, that the robbery had nothing to do with us. I don't think they believed us then, but they left us alone for the rest of the day.

They came to my house and arrested me very early the next morning. It was still dark. I had been sleeping and felt very confused when they took me away.

I saw Steve at the police station. We were kept there for a month. It was very bad there. We were always kept in a small cement cell. It was very crowded and it smelled bad. We were never allowed to go outside. There were older men there, too. We were all kept in there together. Sometimes some of the older men would get angry, and that was very scary. We never knew if they would take their anger out on us.

After one month, we were brought to this prison.

The police discovered who the real burglar was, and they shot him, so now he's dead. But we are still in prison.

My brothers and sisters visit when they can, but that is not very often. They do not have the money for travel. Even with my friend here, I feel very alone.

Sometimes we play football between the cell blocks. We have a ball made out of plastic bags. It passes the time.

I hope I can get out of here soon. When I get out, I want a quiet life with no more life changes. I would like to catch fish and sell them, and be very quiet with the rest of the world.

STEVE, 16

We watch out for each other.

I got as far as grade eight in school. My best subject was English. When I was younger, I wanted to be a soldier when I grew up. I wanted to wear a uniform and carry a gun, march with others, and look very smart and strong. I don't know if that will be possible now. I don't know if they allow people to be soldiers after they've been in prison.

This is what our day is like. When we wake up, we have to wash our plates from the night before, so we are ready to get the day's rations whenever they arrive. We get one meal a day, nsima and beans. We never know when the food will come. Sometimes it comes in the morning, sometimes in the middle of the day, and sometimes at the end. When it comes, we eat. When it doesn't come, we don't.

When the food comes, it is cold, so we have to reheat it over our charcoal brazier. If we don't have charcoal, we burn what we can find, or we eat it cold.

If a visitor comes to see us, we go out to the visiting area to see them. If there is no visitor, we can go outside and play football between the cells.

Sometimes a visitor brings extra food or we get leftover potatoes from the prison farm. We cook these for tea.

We all sleep in one room. Everyone has to sleep on their side, because there is not enough room for anyone to lie flat. We sleep right on the cement. There are not enough blankets. Everyone is supposed to get a blanket. But sometimes, when someone new comes in, there are no extra blankets that day, so there are not enough to go around. We share but sometimes fights break out over who gets a blanket. It's not nice to fight, but when you're cold, you want to be warm.

If you feel sick, you talk to the head of the cell. If he agrees that you're sick, you can go to the clinic. There usually isn't any medicine in the clinic, but sometimes you can sleep for a day or two with a whole blanket to yourself. And you can lie flat out, and that helps.

I don't have a lawyer. Neither does Francis. I don't know how to get one, plus I have no money. I haven't been to court except once, a long time ago. I don't know if the court remembers that Francis and I are here, or if they have forgotten about us, and here is where we will stay, forever and ever.

A preacher comes here sometimes. That's when I feel happy, because we sing and think of better things.

I'm glad I have my friends here, and I've made friends with some of the other boys. There are some of us who don't like fighting, and we watch out for each other.

HOWARD, 13

I just wanted him to leave me alone.

I am charged with murder. I don't think I will ever get out of here. I know of others who are charged with murder, and they have been here a very long time.

There are five children in my family. I got as far as grade seven in school. Both of my parents are alive. My father sells tobacco and my mother sells millet. They set up little stands along the roadside, on pieces of cardboard.

I have been in this place for 16 months. I have never been to court. I don't have a lawyer. My mother and father have no money for a lawyer.

I had an older friend. He was 17. He would fight with this other boy a lot. This other boy was also 17, and a little crazy. He lived with his uncle. His parents were dead. He started going crazy when they were sick, and the sicker they got, the angrier he got. Some of the kids at school said his parents had AIDS, and that made him even angrier. He was always angry, always hitting out at people, at goats, even at trees. He was angry all the time.

I tried to stay away from his anger. I don't like to fight, and I had no disagreement with him. I just wanted him to leave me alone.

But he saw I was friends with the boy he fought with, so he came after me.

He would wait for me after school. Sometimes he'd just watch me, making me afraid. I'd turn around and he'd be there, or I'd have to walk past him and feel him staring at me. Sometimes he'd say things or yell things at me to scare me more. And there were a lot of times when he would beat me. He was much bigger. I tried to fight back, but there wasn't much I could do but let him beat me until he got tired of it.

He would tear up my school books, too, making me get into trouble.

One day he found me on the way to school. He was even angrier than usual. Some of my friends had seen his uncle yell at him and hit him many times. So maybe his uncle had been nasty to him the night before, and that is what made him so angry that morning. I don't know; I have to imagine. He started to yell that he was going to kill me. I yelled back that our families are from the same village, that there was no need for such quarrels. He yelled that he didn't care about that. He was going to kill me anyway. He grabbed for me, but this time I was lucky and got away.

I was really scared. I knew I had to tell somebody, so I ran to the headmaster's office. He took me to my home and told my father what had been happening. My father went to talk to the other boy's uncle. The uncle agreed that it had to end, and that his nephew had to stop bothering me. My father told me that everything would be all right.

The next day was Friday. We had manual labor at our school on Fridays. This meant we all had to bring a tool from home to work in the school garden or to work on repairing things around the school. I carried a hoe.

The older boy found me on the way to school. He was carrying a bicycle chain and a big knife.

He said, "I don't care how much my uncle beats me. I'm not afraid of him. And now I'm going to beat you to a pulp so you'll never be able to talk about me again."

He started to hit me with the bicycle chain. He cut my hand open. He tried to stab me with the knife.

I had my hoe this time to protect myself. He'd try to stab me or hit me with the chain, and I'd swing my hoe to keep him away.

The last time I swung my hoe, it hit him in the head. He dropped to the ground. He didn't get up again. He wasn't dead. He was unconscious.

The noise of our fight had gathered other people. Some people carried him off, and I went home.

He was in the hospital for a week, and then he died.

I went to his funeral. I didn't want him to die. I just wanted him to leave me alone.

His uncle wasn't angry with me. He told my father that the boy had been angry all the time, ever since his parents died. He fought with his uncle over everything. His uncle was sad that he was dead, but he wasn't angry with me.

The boy had relatives in a faraway village. They *were* angry with me. They went to the police, and I was arrested the day after the funeral.

The police came to my house to get me. We don't have a full, real police station in my village—just a small police post. They had no cell to put me in, so they handcuffed me to a stake. I was like that for a whole day, and then I was taken to another police station where they had a proper cell. I spent a month in that cell. Then I was brought here.

My family can't come very often. They have no money, and it makes them feel bad to see me here. I like to see them, but then I feel bad because I can't leave with them when they go back home. Is it better if they forget me, and if I forget them? It hurts to ask myself that.

I don't really have any hope. I will be here until I am very old, and then I will just die.

BABIES

This poem is on the wall of the Open Arms Baby Care Center, Blantyre, Malawi:

AIDS is so limited.
It cannot cripple love.
It cannot shatter hope.
It cannot erode faith.
It cannot take away peace.
It cannot destroy confidence.
It cannot kill friendship.
It cannot shut out memories.
It cannot silence courage.
It cannot invade the soul.
It cannot quench the spirit.
Our greatest enemy is not disease,
But despair.

—AUTHOR UNKNOWN

A young child looks after a baby

On the outskirts of Lilongwe, a short drive into the countryside, there is a village church that doubles as a well-baby clinic. Mothers— and grandmothers—bring their babies to be weighed, vaccinated, and checked by a nurse. While they wait their turn, they sit outside and visit with each other.

EFFIE, 17

I felt old.

Sujakon is my third child. She is two years old. The first child died a week after it was born. I have a little baby, too, who is home today with my mother.

I have never been to school.

The father of my children has left me. We were living together when I had them. We were married. I was happy to get married. I thought my future would be very good, or at least a little bit easier. I thought I wouldn't be hungry so often. I was almost 14.

My husband just got up and left. Maybe he got tired of me. He is a little bit older than I am, and from another village three kilometers away from mine. We got to know each other when we were younger, and became friends. Then we got married. I guess I was too young. I felt old.

I was happy then, but not now. There is no future for me now.

All of my life, I am afraid. I am afraid of hunger, of getting a disease, and of being left alone to cope with hungry, sick children. Sometimes I am able to work a bit, in someone's field, or other work. But not much. I get tired, or I get too sick to work. The children are always there, wanting. Sometimes they are sick, and they want more.

I know about AIDS, but it does me no good to know. I can be

faithful and never be with anyone else. But what about my husband? Now we are separated, and he can be with another woman. What if he comes back and gives me AIDS? What if he has already been unfaithful and has already given me AIDS? There is too much to worry about. I cannot worry about AIDS.

When parents die, the care of their children often falls to the grand-mothers. These brave, amazing women often provide the only hope for the orphans left behind.

ELIZABETH, 50, WITH FELECEY

I don't know what to hope for.

I am 50 years old. Felecey is my granddaughter. She is six weeks old. Her mother, my daughter, died in childbirth. She was sick and weak for a long time before that. I sell vegetables on the street to get a little money. I don't know what to hope for this baby, just that she grows up. The father is in the next village. He helps when he can, but it's not often. He's sick, too.

Elizabeth and Felecey

EVENNESS, 63, WITH ANGELA

I will try.

Angela is a relative of mine, but a very distant relative. Her mother's name was Salina. Salina was already weak from the sickness when she became with child, and got even weaker as the child grew inside her. She died soon after Angela was born. Having the baby took everything out of her.

When some of the relatives saw that Salina was dead and had left

47

Evenness and baby Angela

a tiny baby, they wanted to put the baby into the grave with her. I have heard of such things happening. It is very rare, but if there is no one to care for a baby, people get this idea sometimes. I figured I could take care of her and try to raise her. I bring her to this clinic to get looked at by medical people. To get money for us to live, I sell vegetables by the side of the road.

My hope for Angela is that she will grow well and go to school. It will be hard to pay her school fees. But I will try.

BABIES

- Two-thirds of babies born to HIV-positive mothers do not have HIV themselves.
- HIV-positive mothers can pass the virus on to their babies in the womb, during the birth process, or through breastfeeding.
- Breast milk substitutes require money to buy them and clean water to mix them. Women without these things have to continue breastfeeding.
- Every day 1700 children become HIV-positive.
- HIV-positive babies in developing countries often die early, because their

PART TWO:
Songs of Survival

I don't think the world yet fully appreciates the accelerating and monumental nature of the catastrophe, that what's happening in Africa now may be a harbinger of what is going to happen in South Asia. And if China and India are hit in a similar way, and end up with millions of people between fifteen and forty-nine getting infected with and then dying of AIDS; then we're talking about not just tens of millions, but hundreds of millions of people. How the devil do you deal with it? You've got to put a human face on it!

—STEPHEN LEWIS, *Canadian, UN Special Envoy for HIV/AIDS in Africa*

BEING SICK

The public hospitals in Malawi and Zambia are overcrowded. There are not enough beds, so many patients have to sleep on mats on the floor between the beds. Sometimes patients have to share a single bed with a complete stranger. There aren't enough nurses, because AIDS affects health care workers, too. Family members of the sick person usually stay at the hospital with them, often sleeping under their bed.

PATRICIA, 17

I miss my little boy.

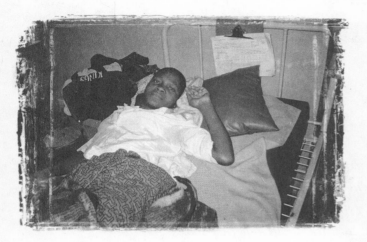

Patricia shows me her knee. On it there is a swelling the size of a softball.

I am from Kambenje Province in Malawi. I have four brothers and sisters, and I am in grade two.

I am sick with a problem with my leg. I have been sick for a long time, in different ways, but now the sickness has taken hold of my leg. I have tuberculosis there. My knee is all swollen. It hurts.

I like to play net ball, but I can't anymore.

They give me liquid antibiotics here, but I don't feel any better yet. I have been sick like this for five months, mostly at home. I got to the hospital a week ago. They say I'll stay another week, then go home again. I hope I am better in a week. I don't think I'll get better at home.

My mother died of the same thing that I have. She was scared before she died, just like I'm scared now.

I had a boyfriend for a while. We lived together, but when I started to get sick, he didn't want to be with me anymore. I had a bad rash and sores in my mouth, and I was tired all the time. After he left me, I came back home to live with my mother. She was very sick by then. We both were, but she was sicker. I took care of her until she died, two months after I came back. I washed her and cooked for her and looked after the house.

I wish I had a boyfriend to come and see me in the hospital. None of my friends can come to visit, because our village is too far away from here. My sister is here taking care of me. It's very nice of her, but I think she gets tired of my company. It's boring for her here in the hospital all the time.

I miss my little boy, too. He is two years old. My uncle and aunt are looking after him until I am well again. If I die like my mother did, will he remember me? I don't know how to make sure he remembers me.

When I am well, I would like to go back to school, but first I have to earn the school fees. I have a small business, too, selling old clothes by the side of the road.

ZINENANI, 17

What is the point of being afraid?

Zinenani is sitting in the sun on the grass outside of the hospital. Her mother is beside her. She has a blanket around her shoulders, even though the day is warm. She is listless. Her mother peels a banana for her, but Zinenani holds it without interest.

I have gone as far as grade nine in secondary school. Physical science is my best subject.

My mother has been bringing me to the hospital every now and then for months. I am taking antibiotics. Maybe they will help. Maybe they won't.

I have been sick for a long time. I cough a lot and throw up. I have no interest in food. There are sores on my skin, and my body hurts all over. I have lost a lot of weight, and I don't feel like doing anything. Everything takes a lot of effort, so I don't feel like doing anything. My mother brings me outside to sit in the sun when it is a sunny day. I like being where it's warm. My body doesn't ache so badly then.

I have heard about AIDS. I learned about it in school, and I read about it on billboards. I know that it weakens your body, so that you get sick from other things, like TB. I don't know if I have AIDS. They haven't tested me—or if they have, they haven't told me. There are no drugs here for AIDS, so what does it matter if I have it?

Before I got sick, I liked to play with small children. I wanted to become a teacher for small children. Will that happen? Depends on whether I get better. My father was sick in 1995 the same way I am now. He died, right here in this same hospital. Maybe I will die, too.

"Stop talking like that," her mother scolds. "I've told you before not to think like that. You will get better."

I have one brother and one sister. I'm the oldest. I had a boyfriend once, but we split up. Actually, my mother chased him away. She said I was too young.

What am I afraid of? Nothing. What's the point of being afraid? Being afraid doesn't stop bad things from happening.

SIGNS AND SYMPTONS OF AIDS

- feeling tired all the time
- ongoing fever, chills, and night sweats
- weight loss
- swollen lymph nodes in the neck, groin, and armpits
- diarrhea, lasting a long time
- unexplained bleeding
- pink or dark purple raised blotches on the skin
- a rash in the mouth, called oral thrush, which makes swallowing painful
- confusion
- body aches
- persistent dry cough

Many people with HIV feel isolated and alone. People know when they're being treated differently. Don't be afraid to reach out.

—MAGIC JOHNSON,
American basketball player, who is HIV-positive

PEER COUNSELING

Peer counseling is a tool being used in many countries. It involves young people reaching out to other young people and providing a safe place where honest talk can happen.

Grace and Elizabeth are peer counselors at the Kara Counseling Center in Lusaka, which specializes in providing services to people with HIV/AIDS. They work in a very crowded, poor part of the city, where shacks are pressed up against one another. The place is full of noise and confusion.

GRACE, 19

It wasn't easy for me to be open.

I never expected to do this type of work. I planned to get married, and that would be my life. But just before I was married, my boyfriend asked me to get my blood tested. I found out then that I'm HIV-positive. My boyfriend dropped me right there and then. I was heartbroken for a while, but you learn to move on.

I have a young daughter. I haven't had her blood tested. I will wait until she's older, and then let her decide for herself whether or not she will be tested. She's healthy right now. Whatever happens in her life, she'll know that I am with her, and that I love her.

I'm open about being HIV-positive now. I do interviews on the radio and for newspapers, and give talks in churches. Most people are not open about being HIV-positive.

Grace and Liz

There's a lot of discrimination. It wasn't easy for me to be open about it. My family gave me my own cup, my own soap, my own toothpaste, and told me not to use anyone else's. They wouldn't let me cook. They didn't understand that AIDS is not spread that way. Some of my friends stopped being my friends. Some stayed with me. And I made new friends. It's possible to be HIV-positive and still have a good life.

At this counseling center, we see a lot of girls who have been raped. It's a story we hear over and over again. The parents die, or one parent dies, and the children are left with relatives while the other parent goes away to earn money. The uncle or older boys or neighbors abuse the children.

This counseling center is in a poor neighborhood. No one has any extra anything—money, food, or space. There are many widows and many orphans. I'd say that at least three-quarters of the orphans are AIDS orphans. Many of them could also be HIV-positive, but they're not tested, so we don't know for sure. Even if they are tested, they can't afford drugs. Here the really poor people eat only one meal a day. They don't have real jobs. They try to sell things in the market. The women who don't have anyone to leave their children with take them along to the market, no matter what the weather. Those children really suffer.

Sometimes a mom or an aunt or grandmother will bring a small child in to us if they think she has been sexually abused. We use dolls to help her tell us what happened. The girl will put one doll on top of another. If the child gets hit at home, she'll make one doll hit the other.

Sometimes family members will know a child has been sexually abused but won't bring her—or him—in for counseling or a check-up because of the shame they feel, especially if the abuser is a relative. And if the abuser is also the breadwinner, the child has no chance.

LIZ, 18

We look normal.

I'm HIV-positive as well. When people come in for testing and we tell them our status, they feel more comfortable talking to us. We look normal—in fact, I think we look beautiful!—so they stop being so afraid and are able to talk easier.

I'm not fully out in the open with my family about my HIV-positive status yet. Not everyone knows. My sister is a nurse and she knows. She was shocked and didn't talk to me for three days when she first heard, but she's been very supportive since then. She just needed some time to get over the shock. I can certainly understand that.

I still have bad days when I am sad about what's happened to me, but I fight it. Sadness can be like an illness itself; if it gets a grip on you, it's hard to get rid of. For people who are HIV-positive, sadness can actually make you sick. When we feel sad, we are more likely to get infections and illness. I don't know why, but it's true. So I keep focused on good things—like our work here, and all the things I like about being alive—and that chases the sadness away.

We also speak at schools. We encourage students to come here for AIDS testing. From age 16 on, a student can get tested without his or her parents' consent. If a woman is married, she doesn't need her husband's consent to be tested. It's all confidential. We've met girls as young as 15 who are widowed because of AIDS. We make sure they understand what is happening to them before we test them.

The most important thing to get across to young people is that they should respect themselves and know that they have rights as human beings. Even if they are HIV-positive, they can still lead proud, strong lives.

Anti-AIDS pamphlets

GIRLS AND AIDS

- Girls and women are two to three times more likely to get HIV than men.

- A woman is twice as likely to get HIV from a man as he is to get it from her.

- There are 12 million HIV-positive women in Sub-Saharan Africa, and 10 million HIV-positive men.

- Women and girls often do not feel powerful enough to demand respect, safety, and protection from their partners.

- Around the world, the notion of "being a man" is often tied in with having many girlfriends, which spreads infections.

- When women and girls are considered to be less valuable than men and boys, they are less likely to get health care when they need it.

- Women without money often have to stay with men who abuse them and cheat on them.

- Nearly 20% of all diseases in women in poor countries between ages 15 and 45 are a result of rape and other forms of male violence.

Pounding corn for nsima

Many people suffering from AIDS are not killed by the disease itself, they are killed by the stigma surrounding everybody who has HIV/AIDS …. We must, therefore, tackle the stigma and discrimination with great urgency. We must show that we care for all those infected by this terrible disease, and we are doing something about it ….

You must not be ashamed of speaking out and telling the community, 'I suffer from HIV/AIDS.' There is no reason, whatsoever, that sufferers should hide that they have been affected by this pandemic. Because when you keep quiet, you are signing your own death warrant.

—NELSON MANDELA,
Former president, South Africa

Your silence will not protect you.

—AUDRE LORDE, *American poet*

Children and leaders of the NAPAM Youth Group

LIVING

There is a street in Lilongwe that is entirely made up of coffin shops. All along the road, men and boys use simple hand tools to shape plain wood into coffins. The finished products are stacked up outside for people to admire. All day long, pickup trucks with singing women in the back load up coffins to take to funerals.

Not far from this street sits the headquarters for the National Association of People with AIDS, Malawi (NAPAM). Along with their families, people who have tested positive for HIV come to the center to get information, find friends, and join in the work of informing others about AIDS.

One Saturday afternoon at NAPAM headquarters, while their parents are inside talking about nutrition, I spend some time hanging out with the children. We play games and sing. And some of them tell me about their lives.

LOTI, 13

I'd like to drive and drive and drive.

I am here with my mother. She comes to learn how to live with AIDS.

I am in grade four. Chichewa language and math are my best subjects. When I don't have to study or do chores, I like to read. If I need to feel better, sometimes I pray, too. When I get together with my friends, we really like to play football. I'm pretty good at it. We all are, really.

My mother has her own business. She sells beer. There are five boys in my family. I am in the middle. My older brothers get to tell me what to do, and I get to tell the younger ones what to do.

My father is a carpenter. My mother wants him to come to NAPAM meetings, but he won't. He makes furniture and coffins. My father says coffins are a kind of furniture. You rest on a chair or a bed, and you rest in a coffin, too.

When I finish school, I would like to be a secretary and work in an office. Working as a secretary is a very important job. You have to keep everything organized. You sit at a desk and people come to you and say, "I need this piece of paper," and you have to know exactly where to find it. I think I would be good at that, and I'd like to have my own desk to work at.

The thing that would make me the most happy would be to own my own car. I'd like to drive and drive and drive, all the way to South Africa.

The only thing that makes me scared is the lack of money. Sometimes my mother and father are too sick to work, and there's no money for food—that scares me. So I want to finish school and have a good job, and be good at my job, so that I'll always have money.

CHOSADZIWA, 13

Here, we learn how to love.

I'm in grade four. English language is my favorite thing to study. The thing I don't really like is science, but they make us do it anyway. It's boring.

There are two children in my family. I'm the oldest and I have a younger brother. He doesn't bother me too much.

My mother stays at home. My father is a guard.

My aunt brought me here today. She comes here to be with good people and to learn how to stay healthy. She says all the people who come here are very good people, and she wants me to be around them.

She told me that other young people like me come here to learn about AIDS, and would I like to join them? I said yes. I come here with her every week.

We learn about the facts of AIDS at school—how we can die from it, how we should not share razor blades or be promiscuous. We learn facts, but we don't learn how to love at school.

Here, we learn how to love.

Because I come here, now I know a lot of people who have HIV. My aunt is HIV-positive. She says she's always been a positive person, and now she's living positively! My aunt makes a lot of jokes like that. Some are funnier than others.

I get happy when I learn more things. I get happy when I spend time with my aunt. I love her, and she loves me.

The only thing that makes me afraid is AIDS.

No, I don't have a boyfriend! What do I need a boyfriend for? I have enough to do.

SOPHILET, 10

I feel good when I'm with my friends.

I am in grade three. English language and math are my best subjects. Reading is my worst.

I like coming to NAPAM on Saturdays. It's like a little party every week. We play and sing and pray and play some more. We practice our English and learn lots of things. The people here are kind to me and kind to each other, which is very nice to see.

Both my mother and father are here. They say this is a good way to keep feeling good. I feel good when I'm with my friends. Sometimes, we start laughing and we can't stop.

My father sells ground nuts on the street. My mother sells charcoal, and that is how we live. I have three brothers and sisters. I am the third child.

When I grow up I would like to be a nurse so I can help heal sick people. My mother and father get sick sometimes, and I would like to know how to make them feel better.

I've been sick, too. I was in the hospital. I don't know what I was sick with. I was just sick.

The thing that would make me happiest would be if I could heal people. That would really be wonderful.

ARIX, 7

It would make me happy to be a kind man.

I have two sisters and three brothers. I am the second boy. My father brought me here. He said everybody at NAPAM is kind, and I need to learn how to grow into a kind man. It would make me happy to be a kind man, and also to have my own car.

ERNEST, 9

I'm good at everything.

My favorite thing is learning new things. I come to NAPAM to learn and to play.

I would like to be a truck driver when I grow up. It's just an ambition. I don't know if I can make it happen but I think I can. I would be bigger then, of course. You have to be a big man to be able to drive a big truck.

My father died of AIDS. My mother brings me here. First we all sit together and pray and sing and hear about things from the Bible. Then she has to stay inside with the other adults and talk some more. I get to come outside and play and be with other children.

My mother takes good care of me. She keeps saying, "Did you eat some fruit today? Did you eat some vegetables?" She makes me eat them even when I don't like them. I argue with her, but she keeps making me. That's how she takes care of me.

My favorite meal is nsima with meat. We don't have meat very often, so I usually eat nsima with beans, which is all right, too.

I'm in grade three. I'm good at everything. Nothing scares me. I'm smart, and I'm brave.

YAMIKANI, 12

I would like to be ready for death.

I come to NAPAM to learn about AIDS and to be with other kids who also want to learn about AIDS. It makes me happy to be here. They let us talk about the things we are worried about.

Some of the things we learn are the same as we learn at school, but here we are also able to support each other. We learn that we can ask for support if we need it, and we learn that we can give support if someone needs us.

Here we talk to each other, learn who we are, study things from the Bible, and learn about kindness and love.

Most of the adults who come here are HIV-positive, because it's a place for people who are living with AIDS. It's about *living* with AIDS, not *dying* with AIDS. Do you understand the difference?

One of the things I think about a lot is death. I wonder about dying. Am I going to die young or not? What will happen when I die? Will I know what to do when the time comes? The books don't tell you how to die. How will I know when it's time?

I see other people going to the graveyard, and I wonder how they died. Did they find it hard to die? Were they good people? Did they live a right life or a wrong life? Were they afraid? I wonder.

Sometimes I wish they could sit up and tell me what it is like to die. That is something I need to know, so that I can be ready. I like to be ready for a test at school. I would like to be ready for death, too.

You can't tell by looking at someone if they have HIV. Some of the children here have HIV in their blood. I know who some of them are, but not all of them. They don't all know, because not everyone has been tested. I'm not going to tell you if I'm HIV-positive or not. We are all the same.

I'm going to sing you an AIDS song now:

Boys and girls are dying from AIDS.
Parents are dying from AIDS.
We must all fight against AIDS.

I would like to be a musician when I grow up, especially a rich musician. I could sing songs about AIDS and also spiritual songs. I will be very rich and very famous, and then maybe I won't think about death anymore.

NAMITSO, 14

I fed my mother first.

My father is alive but he is away a lot. He is a mechanic and lives somewhere else. I live with relatives. I come here to learn how to prevent HIV/AIDS. I also come here because it is somewhere to go, somewhere where people care about me and want to know how I am and what I'm doing.

I am in grade five. Math is my best subject. I would like to be a minibus driver when I grow up, so that I can see other places.

My mother died last year. She had TB. She also had AIDS, which made the TB stronger. She was sick for eight months. She got weaker and weaker.

She was in the hospital for a long time. I was the one who took care of her in the hospital. There was a nurse, but she was too busy to do much for my mother. I had to do it.

I stayed in the hospital with her. I slept on the floor, under her bed. The ward was crowded, even the floors, and that was the only spot I could find. I did what I could for her. She didn't want to eat, but I made her eat. She was weak, so I took food to her lips and made her eat.

Sometimes my father would be around, and he would bring food to the hospital. Then we would have extra things to eat, like fruit.

Usually we had to eat what the hospital brought, which was nsima and beans. I fed my mother first. Whatever she could not eat, that's what I ate.

I washed our clothes in the sink in the ward and spread them out in the sun to dry. One of the other women, who was looking after someone else, showed me how. Sometimes she let me use her soap, but not very often because she was poor, too. But I washed things out with water, and the sun helped make them clean.

There were a lot of very sick people at the hospital. That's what a hospital is for. Most people had someone like me with them—a mother, aunt, son, or daughter. We all slept on the floor, under the beds.

I learned how to care for other people, not just my mother. Sometimes a patient had no family to care for them. The rest of us would help that person out.

I saw a lot of people die. They'd die, and they'd be carried out. Their bed would soon be used by somebody else. The dead person just went away.

Some people couldn't eat, and I helped them eat. Some people cried all night. Sometimes I would sit with them so they didn't feel alone. Sometimes I tried to cover my ears because I didn't want to hear their cries.

I learned how to love people, by taking care of my mother.

I was afraid a lot of the time. I was the only one around to take care of my mother, and I didn't really know how. The nurse helped me when she could, and other patients' families helped, but I was still afraid I would do something wrong and make her die.

She did die, but people told me it was not my fault.

The best thing I get at NAPAM is encouragement. The people here like me, and they tell me to do good things in my life. That's why I like to come here. There are people here who are keeping track of me. It makes me want to grow up to be a good man.

A village chief in Malawi with some of the children she cares for

PART THREE:
Songs of Victory

HIV is the start of the next phase of your life. Don't lose hope, and don't give up. You're still a normal person, and you can still do a lot of the same things you did before.

—MAGIC JOHNSON,
American basketball player, who is HIV-positive

When the Scots came to Malawi in the 1800s, they brought their religion with them. The Established Church of Scotland changed its name to the Church of Central African Presbyterian (CCAP). There are still CCAP churches all over Malawi.

The bus station is a short walk from the youth hostel where I'm staying. Here children gather around the water pump to get their families' supply. I make my way through the friendly chaos of the station to an old CCAP church. It was built by the missionaries who settled here. Other buildings are on the large, leafy mission grounds. One of them is a private school.

Ramsy and Marantha are students in the senior school.

RAMSY, 17

My parents are very smart people.

I'm a good student. I take my schoolwork very seriously because it is the best chance for me to have a good life. I consider school to be my job for now. Both my parents have jobs. My father is a building contractor. My mother runs a small business.

My father's sister died of AIDS. My aunt was sick for a long time—in the hospital, then home again, then back in the hospital again. When she went into the hospital for the last time, she was in for a long while. I went to visit her but not very often. I wish now I had gone to see her more, but it frightened me to see her like that, so ill. There was less of her every time I saw her. Her face looked old. Even her voice was old. It made me very sad and afraid to see her like that. I decided I could not go there again. She died a little while after that.

I decided not to go to the funeral. I was too sad to go. My brothers went, though. They told me there was conflict among the relatives about how my aunt died. My father told us clearly that she had AIDS. My parents are very smart people and believe in telling the truth, so my father was very honest about this. A lot of the relatives didn't want to hear this, and they argued with him. They were arguing right at the funeral! The relatives said my father was bringing shame on the family. My father said that my aunt was a good person, and we wouldn't be respecting her if we lied about her.

I'm glad I wasn't there. I liked my aunt very much. She was always kind to me. I don't like thinking of her being so sick, and now being dead. I would not have liked to hear people fighting at her burial.

My aunt was a teacher in a government school. She left behind three children. My cousins are 15, 11, and 7. They are orphans now. They should have been kept together, but they were split up. Each one is being cared for by a different relative. I'm not able to see them. They're not in Blantyre anymore.

Their father, my aunt's husband, is alive. But he is not around. No one here has seen him since the funeral. He has another wife and children in a northern village. So my aunt's children have lost both their parents. If he gave AIDS to my aunt, he's probably given it to his other wife, too.

A lot of people in Malawi don't like to talk about AIDS. If they do talk about it, AIDS happens in other families, not their own.

We hear a lot about AIDS in school. We have an anti-AIDS club. A lot of schools have them. We do fun things like put on plays and go on trips. We're told that both boys and girls should be proud to be virgins, and it's better to concentrate on our studies and on sports. It's a good message, and one that every student in this school could recite. But real life is sometimes more complicated. Sometimes people get lonely or sad—or they like each other and just forget about slogans.

I would like to do well enough in school to be able to go to university. I'd like to be a doctor, not just because I watched my aunt die but because I would like to do something good in the world.

Malawi is a small country, but our people are as strong and as smart as people from big, important countries. I would like to prove this is true.

MARANTHA, 15

How will I know?

I was made a school prefect just two days ago. I was very pleased to be asked. It's a position that carries a lot of responsibility because prefects help run the school. I guess the teachers saw something in me that made them think I'd be good at this job—maybe because I'm so entertaining.

Everyone at this school has been affected by AIDS. You could ask any child here. I know we all look like normal children, but we all have a story.

People with AIDS are really looked down on, like they're bad people. People who once were their friends suddenly want nothing to do with them. Their families often abandon them, too. Dying is bad enough, but they're dying alone. I can't think of anything worse than that.

My aunt is seriously ill. I guess it's not really polite to say why, but I'll say it anyway, because keeping a secret is not good. She has AIDS. She went to have a blood test because she had been feeling sick for a long time. Her husband has AIDS, too, but he is not so sick. They don't have any children. I guess that is a good thing. My mother and father have gone to visit her. She lives in a village not far from Blantyre.

A lot of AIDS is spread by the husband not taking very good care of his wife. He might get the disease somewhere else, and then give it to his wife and children. A lot of people die that way, especially children. He gives it to his wife, and his wife gets sick and has babies who are also sick. A lot of babies die that way.

You can't tell if someone is HIV-positive. They can look and feel healthy for a long time. The teachers here have told us this. What they don't tell us is how to find a husband you can trust. My uncle is a good man, and he still gave AIDS to my aunt. How will I know that the man I marry won't give AIDS to me? The teachers don't tell us that.

With teenagers, AIDS spreads because they try to experience things. They don't feel strong enough in themselves to do other, better things with their time. A lot of them don't feel loved by their families, and they look for love in other places. And then they become sick.

Parents should love their children and treat them right so that the children don't have to look for other people to love them.

The last thing I want in my life right now is a boyfriend. Girls who get into relationships with boys always lose themselves. Sometimes I can barely recognize them anymore because they change themselves so much, hoping the boy will like them. The boys push them to go further and further. And the girls want to be liked, so they go along. Then they get sick or have other troubles.

That's why I'm so glad to be a prefect. It's a good challenge. You have to do things with a kind heart, because even if you catch somebody doing something they shouldn't, they're still a good person. I will work very hard to do this job well and not disappoint anybody, especially myself.

I think the difference between teenagers who feel good about themselves and those who don't is their parents. A lot of parents don't talk with their teenagers, so their children don't have anywhere to turn if there's a problem. People think, What problems can children have? They're small people, so they have small problems. But if kids know their parents can solve the small problems, they'll trust their parents to help with the big ones.

A lot of kids don't think they have any value, because their parents don't treat them well. So they go with people who pretend to like them. They don't have any way to tell the good people from the bad people. They don't think they are worth anything, so it doesn't matter how they are treated.

My greatest fear is that I'll lose one or both of my parents. I can tell them anything—so can my brothers and sisters. I'm always eager to see them, every day. We all like being with each other.

Mealtime at Mulanje orphan care center

I have many things I want to do in my life, including becoming a doctor. I know my family is behind me. That makes me strong.

Members of the Anti-AIDS Club

Light tomorrow with today.

—ELIZABETH BARRETT BROWNING,
English Poet

ANTI-AIDS CLUBS

NCHINUNYA, 16

I'm happiest when I'm at school.

I live with my uncle. My mother died in 1995, my father in 1997. They died from AIDS.

Life with my uncle is okay. One of my brothers is living there with me. My uncle is a soldier, so we see more of our aunt.

I'm happiest when I'm at school. I like civics and science the best, because it's good to know how things work—especially the government. I'd like to be an accountant when I leave school because it would be good, steady work.

The Anti-AIDS Club helps keep me focused on the important things. I'm not tempted to do drugs or have boyfriends, but it's good to be with other kids who think like I do. It keeps me strong.

OSWARD, 16

I've known a lot of sadness.

It's difficult to define what it means to be a man, especially what it means to be a good man. We get a lot of mixed messages, such as to be a man means to go with a lot of women and to make women do things for us. Some men beat up on women and also on smaller men. That's not the kind of man I want to be.

My father died a long time ago, so I have to look for other examples of how to be a man. I only have one life, and I want to live it doing things that I am proud of. Sometimes that means I feel alone, separate from other men.

I've known a lot of sadness. Both of my parents are dead, and two of the children in my family have died, all from AIDS. I pray when I get sad, and I try to put the sadness behind me.

A lot of children in Zambia have a much harder life than I do. They are forced to do hard manual labor, like working in the fields or breaking stones in a quarry. I want to be able to help those kids, so I study hard in school and try to grow up smart and strong. My favorite subjects are Zambian and world history.

Being part of the Anti-AIDS Club is a statement. It tells people who I am.

We try to create a good space for ourselves with the club, because outside of this space, the world is not good. The girls in our school often get bothered by men in the neighborhood, and the smaller boys get threatened by bigger boys who are not in school and are jealous of those who are. We see prostitutes and other people who commit crimes because they are angry and hungry. And beyond our neighborhood, beyond Lusaka, beyond Zambia even, there are wars and bad things happening—often to children. So we try to make a place where we can be safe and strong, have good values, and feel good about being ourselves.

Maybe throughout my life I can create my own definition of being a man.

Children putting on an anti-AIDS play

As sport responds to the call to fight AIDS, it's imperative that sport leaders understand that to get to the root cause of the AIDS epidemic will require for a start cancellation of foreign debt, reversal of poverty, fight against corruption, and also solidarity for social justice. As many have echoed, this fight also requires that we act locally and think globally.

—Oscar Sichikolo Mwaanga,
Zambian, president of Edusport

KICKING AIDS OUT

The Edusport office is on the edge of the downtown section of Lusaka. The office towers are in one direction, the Great Plains in another. This is where I meet Brenda.

BRENDA, 18

You want to respect yourself.

I've been involved with Edusport for over a year. We do much more than sports. We build leaders and communities.

We have a project called Kicking AIDS Out, which combines AIDS education with games, to get kids active and able to talk about subjects they can't usually talk about at home. We have a girls' empowerment project called Go Sister! We have a project called POWER, which stands for People Organizing and Working for Economic Rebirth. It gives small loans to poor farmers, who repay the loans and also give back by doing HIV support activities

Brenda and a friend from Edusport

75

as part of the loan agreement. AID Yourself sends teams into the slums to clean up the area. This cuts down on cholera in the rainy season, and builds pride in our homes.

When kids come into Edusport, they're put into a team and everyone is given a tree to plant. Zambia has problems with deforestation, so we plant trees and each kid is responsible for keeping their tree alive.

So, as you can see, we do much more than sports. But sports are the foundation.

My father died in 1998 of TB. I don't know if he was also HIV-positive or not, since he wasn't tested for that, but a lot of people with TB also have AIDS.

My mother disappeared seven months ago. She was also in the hospital with TB. She had a small business selling things by the road, but the people who looked after it for her while she was sick stole her money. She left the hospital to find out about it, even though she was too sick to be out. We haven't heard from her since. This was in another province. I don't know where she is now. I don't think she can get to us, or she would have come here by now.

I completed high school a short while ago. This week or next week, I go to the Social Work School at the University of Zambia for six months on an Edusport scholarship. Edusport paid my high school fees, too, in exchange for my coaching.

Sports are important, especially for girls. It is still a fairly new thing for girls to be involved in sports in Zambia. People consider it unladylike. They say, "She's trying to act like a boy," and "All that jumping around is bad for her." But it's important for girls to know they can be strong and fast.

The coach-training program starts when kids are quite young. We train both girls and boys to be coaches. The girls will coach both boys' and girls' teams. Imagine what that does—when girls have the strength and skills to coach the boys, and the boys learn to take direction from girls. It teaches girls to be assertive and to have self-esteem. And it teaches boys to think about girls in a new way, a respectful way.

Basketball is my game. I even got to go to Zimbabwe to play. It's a struggle, though. For one thing, my church thinks women should only wear skirts. You can't play sports in a skirt, so there are people at church who look down at me. But I love sports, and I won't give them up just to please other people.

I have other problems when I go to matches. It's hard to get money from my brother for the train fare. Also, sometimes the train comes back at six or seven in the evening, and my brother says things like, "A lady should be home by five," which doesn't even make sense. He says, "You're only doing this to meet boys." He knows that's not true. He just says it to make me angry, to show he has more power than I do. At least, he thinks he does.

Money is very hard. We own our own house, so we're lucky. But we have to rent it all out and live in a shed at the back of the yard. There's me, my brother, and my two younger sisters. My brother takes all the rent money and keeps it. I had to go to the police to get him to give us money for school. We run out of food a lot. Sometimes the tenants buy us a bag of mealie meal (cornmeal) instead of paying the full rent in cash. My brother doesn't like that, but at least we eat.

I want to get some money from my brother to go look for our mother, so she can come home and solve our problems. My brother says we don't even know where she is, so it would be a waste of money. I hope she's all right. I hope she comes back to us.

I was picked under the United Nations to be part of the National Measles Campaign. I conducted a three-day workshop in Luapula Province, and then went back again later to help nurses mobilize children for vaccines.

I also went back for one week for a sports health festival. We used sports as a tool to persuade kids to get the vaccine and take care of their health. We gave out some balls and Frisbees, and played games with the kids. We also taught some of the kids how to organize games.

I hope my sisters get involved in sports. It will make them

stronger and give them the confidence they need to stand up to the men in their lives.

Sports make you want to take care of your body. You want to respect yourself and have other people respect you. You don't want to settle for anything less.

A gift of soap

If I had a song,
I'd sing it in the morning
I'd sing it in the evening
All over this land.

— PETE SEEGER,
American folk musician and songwriter

ARTS AGAINST AIDS

In Mulanje, there's a party in the clearing. Children stream in from the bush—a constant stream of orphans flowing in from all sides. There is a lot of laughter and excitement. After some singing, the clearing goes quiet as the ground fills up with children sitting and eating from plates of nsima and beans. The excitement starts up again when boxes full of bars of soap are brought out. Volunteers help the children line up, and everyone gets a bar. I've never seen children so happy to get soap.

Members of the Last Message

But the party's not over yet. The children are entertained with plays, poetry, and the music of a rock band.

One of the rock band members has an old electric guitar. They take the battery out of a pickup truck, and hook the amplifier up to it. The music cuts in and out, as the connections to the battery slip on and off, but that doesn't stop the dancing.

The plays the children put on are without scripts. They rehearse a bit beforehand, but the dialogue is made up as they go along. They make their characters come alive without props or costumes, and had us all spellbound with their performance.

CHRISTOPHER, 13

We write our own music.

I live in Mulanje. The name of our band is The Last Message. It means that our message, which is to end HIV, is the last message; because if we don't end it, it will be the last of us. How could our band not have an anti-AIDS message? We have seen how the disease goes, what it does to people, how sad it makes our people. Of course, we have to sing about it.

I started making music in church, singing with the choir. Music makes me feel powerful. Plus, it's fun. I play the guitar. It is an electric guitar, but usually I play it without electricity. I have a friend named Felix who taught me to play. It's really his guitar, but he lets me use it.

We write our own music. We usually write our songs together. One of us will get an idea, and we all work on it, changing words and parts of the tune until we have a song that we're all happy with. Sometimes we even rewrite a song after we've performed it in public.

My father died when I was a baby. My mother died when I was a little older. They may have died of AIDS. I'm not sure. The doctor didn't test their blood because there were no drugs for them anyway, so he just tried to make them feel better. My aunt takes care of me now.

The thing I like best in the world is football. I would like to be a professional football player when I grow up. Or maybe do something with computers.

CHRIS, 16

They are happy for a while.

I play the drums in our group. I built them myself. For the drum heads, I found some old tin cans and put cow skins across them. For cymbals, I strung beer-bottle caps together. They make a pretty good sound.

I also like football, but I would rather be a musician, especially a keyboard musician. I don't know how to play the keyboard, and I don't know anyone who has one. But someday I'll learn.

Both my mother and father are alive, but I know a lot of kids who are orphans. It must be a very sad thing to lose your parents. You would feel lonely forever.

We came here today to give an anti-AIDS message, but mostly we came here to entertain. It doesn't fix anything, but if people enjoy us, they are happy for a while. Did you see how everybody was dancing, even the smallest kids?

I think we made them happy. That makes me feel good. It has been a good day.

GHOSTA, 14

All my friends have lost their parents.

I love being in plays. I love pretending to be someone else. I feel like I'm in a whole different world when I do. I don't get nervous at all. I'm a natural actor. I especially love it when I make people laugh.

I also love singing, dancing, and playing football.

My mother died first, when I was 8. My father died when I was 11. I don't remember much about my mother dying. I do remember that she used to take care of me.

I live with my grandmother now. I call her Gogo. That's what we usually call our grandmothers. I live there with three of my sisters and brothers. My oldest sister lives in Blantyre with an uncle.

My grandmother makes her living by making beer and selling it. I help her. We make it at our house, and this is how we do it: we get sugar and then we soak it in water with maize husks. We leave it for four days, then take the husks out with a sieve, boil the soaking water, then put it into a still. After a while, the beer comes out of the still. It's clear, like water, but it's not like water when you drink it! I don't drink it, though. I just help her make it and sell it.

My grandmother built the still herself. It's made of wood and bits of old pipe. She's very clever.

My father died at our house in 2000. Gogo looked after him. He got very sick first. He was sick for a long time. I helped by bathing him when he became too weak to wash himself, and I helped him get to the toilet. I'd feed him, too, when he couldn't feed himself. I'd feed him porridge in the morning and nsima in the evening. He was very, very thin when he died.

He used to talk to me when we were together like that. He told me about what his life was like when he was my age, and how proud he was of me, and how I should stay in school after he died. He knew he was going to die, because he had the same thing that killed my mother. It made him very unhappy. He said he wanted to stay alive so that he could watch me grow. But he also said that when he died, he'd still be watching me from heaven. I try to behave properly now, so he will be pleased with me.

I had a lot of stomach problems after he died. I couldn't eat much, and I felt bad for a very long time. I was at his funeral. It was very sad, especially when I saw a lot of grown-ups crying. I cried, too.

That's why I like to sing so much now and entertain people.

There are a lot of kids here who have lost somebody, and grown people have lost someone, too. Kids lose older people, and older people lose their kids. That's a lot of sadness. If I can make them happy with my singing—even for a little while—that's a very good thing.

In Gogo's house, I have a regular bed with a mattress. Some people just sleep on the floor, but we don't. I get up just before six, sweep the ground outside, build up the fire, get water and wash, go to school, and then come back here to the Orphan Club.

My friend and I know about AIDS. We put on plays about it. We know we can get it if we sleep around and allow older men to give us money to do things to our bodies. We have to take care of ourselves. All my friends have lost their parents. We talk about it among ourselves—what it's like to be orphans, what we're going through. We help each other out. We've become a new family for each other.

The only thing I fear is God. We must respect God, because He decides everything.

ROBERT, 13

He wanted to be sure we would remember him.

I am in grade seven. I live in Chita village with my Aunt Mary. My two brothers also live there. I am the oldest.

I like to be in plays, but I like singing even more. Sometimes we sing about AIDS or about being orphans. Sometimes we just sing happy songs about the world and being alive. I would like to be a professional singer when I get older, especially gospel music. It makes me happy all over when I sing.

I was eight years old when my mother died. She had something wrong with her stomach, I think. She had sores in her mouth and on her face, and she couldn't eat. She got thinner and thinner. She was sick for a long time. My Aunt Mary took care of her. Mom kept telling us to stay in school, and not be with girls so that we wouldn't get what she got. It's good advice, although I didn't really understand it at the time.

I don't know if she knew she was dying. Maybe she did, because she kept giving us advice about how to live. I do know that she was very scared. But just being sick can make a person scared.

My father died two years after my mother's death. He was sick in the same way my mother was. He had bad headaches and had sores on his skin. By the time he died, he was very skinny, too. When he started getting that skinny look, I was pretty sure he was dying, just like my mother. But I hoped I was wrong. Then he started giving us advice, the way she did, and I knew for sure that he was going to die. He talked with us about taking care of ourselves and staying in school. I think he was sad to be leaving us. He wanted to be sure we would remember him.

I am healthy, I think. I have a scar on my knee from when I fell off my bicycle. I was taking a load of wood to the market, and I put too much wood on. The bike was too heavy, and I couldn't control it, so I fell off. But other than that, I am well.

AIDS scares me a lot. AIDS and robbers. A lot of people are robbed. The robbers come in the night and take things when you are asleep. They steal because they have no money. But it's still bad.

I want to keep singing all my life. Maybe I could make a recording someday. Some things will try to get in the way of me being a success, but I won't let them.

On a cold, damp Sunday in Lilongwe, people gather in the auditorium of the teachers' college. We are bundled up against the cold, and we keep our coats on because the auditorium is unheated. Lively music comes over the loudspeaker, and onto the stage in a swirl of energy runs the Anglican Voices Choir. Soon the whole audience is dancing and singing with them.

Left to right: *Nedia, Dave, and the choirmaster from Anglican Voices*

NEDIA, 13

Our music might help them to feel better.

I have been singing with the Anglican Voices Choir for two years. I heard them when I was younger and thought it would be fun to sing with them, so I joined.

I am in the ninth grade. I live with my mother and father in Diante, outside Blantyre. My father works as a driver. My mother stays at home and takes care of us.

There is a lot of suffering right now in Malawi. A lot of people are poor. A lot of people have AIDS and other diseases. When people suffer, they are unhappy. And when they are unhappy, they suffer more.

I think about that suffering when we are singing, like I do today. We are here in the hall of the teachers' college, and people have come from all around Lilongwe to hear us. Maybe there are people hearing us today who are having a really bad day. Maybe they have no money and are hungry; maybe they have someone they love at home who is very sick or has just died; or maybe they are dying themselves and they are sad about that. Our music might help them feel better.

The words of the songs—I like them, too. They are about praising God and turning to God when we are in trouble. The music is lively and with a good beat to it, so you can't help dancing to it.

The thing that makes me happiest, even happier than singing, is net ball. The thing that scares me most is that I might get a disease like AIDS. There is no cure for AIDS. If you get it, first you get very sick, and then you die. Lots of people in Malawi have HIV or AIDS, and they don't even know it. Probably some of the people who came to hear us today have AIDS. They need our music more than anybody.

I would like to be a nurse when I grow up, to help those who get sick with diseases. I'll keep singing, too. I'll be a singing nurse, and I'll cheer people up as I make them feel better. And when they are well, we'll play net ball.

DAVE, 11

Malawi is a beautiful country.

I've been singing forever. I started to sing when I was three years old. I heard other people singing, and they looked like they were having such a good time, I naturally joined in.

I like feeling the music move through me. We have different

dances and moves we do with each song. It's fun to learn them. We get mixed up at first, but that's fun, too. Then, when we all know the moves and we're moving together, it feels great.

My mother and father are still living. We live in Blantyre. I'm lucky. I know lots of kids who have lost their father or mother. They died because they were sick. I don't know if they died of AIDS or not. We don't ask those questions. A lot of people do die of AIDS, but it's not polite to ask. And if someone is already feeling bad, you don't want to make them feel worse.

We perform our music in different places. Our home church is in Blantyre, but we have sung in Mzuzu, in Mangochi, and today in Lilongwe. Malawi is a beautiful country, and I like traveling around and seeing different places.

Wherever we go, people put up posters announcing that we are coming, and the newspapers carry a special announcement, too. I like thinking of people in different places seeing the poster in the market and getting excited because we are coming to their town to sing for them. I imagine them looking forward to it, talking about it with their families over their meal, and making plans to see us. It makes me want to do a good job.

We've recorded a CD, too. That was a lot of fun. I felt like a professional singer. People buy our CD so they can listen to our music when we're not there.

I want to be a professional singer when I grow up, especially singing gospel music. That's what makes me the most happy.

Trendsetters Newspaper, Zambia's leading youth newspaper, is a lively, professional newspaper sold on the streets and in shops. It is bursting with articles on arts, sports, and celebrities such as Cherise, the Zambian woman on the "Big Brother Africa" TV show, and the Zambian performers on "South African Idols," a pop-star show. It also carries serious life and death stories about coping with AIDS, rape, and poverty. *Trendsetters* is a rallying cry, a challenge to Zambian youth to take a full role in the shape of their country, affirming both their right and their ability to do so.

Their offices are on the second floor of a building a short walk from the main street of downtown Lusaka.

PRISCA, 19

We are sure we will live forever.

Our motto is "Setting Trends for a Wise and Proud Generation." Being a journalist is what I've always wanted to do. Some employers won't give young people an opportunity, so we must create our own opportunities.

Our newspaper talks about many issues—music, movies, sports, self-esteem, dating, school, finding a job, getting along with family members—all things that are of interest to young people. And, of course, we write about health, too—reproductive health, Sexually Transmitted Diseases (STDs), and AIDS. But young people don't really think about their health. We are sure we will live forever, so if our newspaper only talked about health issues, no one would read us. So, along with AIDS and other health topics, we write about things that are of immediate concern to our readers.

Our editorial board is made up of young people. These people are the writers, photographers, managers, art directors, editors—everything. It's important that young people be in charge of running a youth paper because, when adults get involved, they tend to be preachy.

When we write about child abuse, we get a lot of letters from readers who realize that the abuse they suffered was not their fault. People are beginning to discuss women's rights and children's rights, and they are realizing they can speak up and fight back.

A lot of kids don't want to get a blood test for HIV/AIDS because they don't want to know. They don't want to think, Hey, I'm 18, and I could be dying. If they do get tested and find out that they are HIV-positive, they have a hard time asking for what they need. There are Youth Friendly Societies in Zambia, which are health clinics for young people, but there are not nearly enough of them. Many adults are so moralistic, are so judging of people who are in trouble.

The life of a young woman in Zambia depends on her circumstances—mostly on how much money her family has. If her family can afford to keep her in school, she has a much better chance at a good life. Schools should be better at teaching young women their rights. Even educated girls don't always feel strong enough to stand up for themselves.

Girls who come from poor families have a very hard time. They have fewer choices, so even if they know their rights, they don't have the power to demand them. And if they have babies when they're still young, they have even fewer choices.

Men still have the idea that women are inferior—that we exist only to serve their needs. That's why AIDS is a women's rights issue. We have to have the right to be able to say who gets to touch us and how. I hope our newspaper can contribute to making that happen.

Women cooking nsima

When I dare to be powerful—
to use my strength in the service of my vision,
then it becomes less and less important
whether I am afraid.

—AUDRE LORDE, *American poet*

STORY WORKSHOP

Since 2000, the radio soap opera "Zimachitika" has been the number one radio play in Malawi. Every week over seven million listeners of all ages tune in. In villages where there is only one radio, the whole village gathers around to hear the adventures of a family as they deal with issues that affect everyone in the country—including AIDS, poverty, and child abuse.

The show is taped on Saturday afternoons in a house in a leafy, green section of Blantyre. A room in the house has been turned into a recording studio. I meet two of the young actors as they are about to record an episode of the drama.

MACFORD, 11

I know children who get hit by their parents.

I live with my mother and father in Naperi, a part of Blantyre near the Malambalala River. I am in the seventh grade at school. English is my best subject. Mathematics is my worst.

I like being on the radio. The character I play is called Tobias, who is a lot like me. The play we are doing today is about family planning. We rehearsed it in the morning, and we'll record it for the radio this afternoon. The boy I play has a rough father. He beats his children. I think he is rough because he has too many children and he is not able to look after them all. He gets upset when they're hungry and he can't feed them, so he beats them.

There are six children in my own family. I'm number four. We have a good father. He doesn't beat us. But I know kids who get hit by their parents. The kids will try to pretend that they're tough, that they don't really care about being hit. But I think they care a lot.

Here is a typical day for me. On a school day, I get up at five in the morning, wash, put on my clothes, drink tea, gather my books, and go to school. I come home in the afternoon and eat lunch, usually nsima. My parents say I should spend the hour between three and four reading a book, so I do. I get books from school or from the library in Blantyre. After reading, I can go out and play. But I must be home by five, before it gets dark. If I have homework, I do that. I have dinner, then go to sleep.

Macford performing on the radio show

My friends and I like to play tennis and football. Sometimes we just run around and laugh. I have a pretty normal life, except that I also get to be on the radio.

In the Story Workshop plays, we talk about serious things. It is fun, but it is also important. Other boys might learn things from Tobias, the character I play, so I try to do a good job.

We talk about AIDS a lot on the show. Sometimes it's the main story, sometimes it's just mentioned, and the main story is about something else. We talk about AIDS a lot because a lot of people in Malawi have it or they at least know someone who has it.

AIDS is a disease that kills people. You can get it if you use a bad needle or if you are promiscuous, which means you have a lot of girl-friends. I can't tell if the people around me have AIDS or not. I'm very afraid of catching AIDS, because then I would die. It's scary to not know if you are beside someone who has it. At school and on the show we're told that you can't catch it just from being around some-body who has it. But it is still scary.

I know someone, a relative, who was sick for a long, long time. He kept getting sicker and sicker and sicker, until he just died. I don't know if he had AIDS or not. No one told me. He started out as a big man. Then each time I saw him, there'd be a little less of him.

When I finish school, I would like to be a lawyer. I think it would be interesting, plus I would get to wear a nice suit and sit behind a big desk.

I had never acted before I got the job at Story Workshop. They chose me from a lot of other kids because I have a good reading voice. It's a lot of fun and I get paid. Some of the money I make goes into the bank, but some I get to spend on things I like, like video games. That's when I'm happiest, when I'm playing video games.

I'm very famous among my friends because I'm on the radio. They're not jealous, though. Well, maybe they are a little envious!

ENELESI, 10

I know I will be good.

I'm here at the Story Workshop to take part in a play for the radio.

There are seven children in my family. I'm number six. My father works at Malawi Telecom Ltd. My mother stays at home and works in the house.

Here is my usual day. I wake up and check to see if the bathroom is free. Usually, though, Dad is in there. So I go out and sweep the yard, which is my chore. When Dad gets out of the bathroom, I go in and wash and put on my school uniform. It is white around the neck, and the rest of it is blue. After I'm dressed I drink tea, and sometimes I have some bread. Sometimes I even have an egg. Then I pick up my book bag and go to school. English is my best subject. My worst is agriculture, where we have to learn about crops and soil. I don't like that.

Enelesi's first radio performance

I know a lot about AIDS. I know you can get it from sharing a razor blade. We talk about it in school, but my friends and I don't talk about it among ourselves. It is a teacher-thing to talk about.

There are children in my class whose parents have died. Actually, there are a lot of children like that. One girl in my class, her name is Violet, has lost both of her parents. I don't know what made them die. She doesn't talk about it. None of the kids whose parents have died talk about it. And my mother says it's not polite to ask.

AIDS is my biggest fear because it can kill you. AIDS and getting pregnant. I don't want either one to happen to me.

I have two brothers. The oldest one is all right, but the youngest one bothers me a lot. We argue about all sorts of things. Here's one of the things we argue about: we buy our bread in plastic bags, and when the bread is finished, we argue about who gets the bag. We roll the empty bags into a ball to play with. My parents say we should save the bags together and make one ball we can both use. But, of course that won't work at all.

With my friends, my favorite game to play is called Fly. In this game, one kid stands on one side, another on the other, and there is someone in the middle. The one in the middle has to try to catch the ball when it is thrown. That is called Fly.

The thing I like best about my life is that I am hardly ever sick. I know lots of people who get sick a lot, and I am glad to not be one of them.

My sister gets sick a lot. She is in my class at school even though she is older. This is because she is sick so much. I don't know what's wrong with her. My parents won't say. When I ask them, their faces get sad, so I don't ask them. Sometimes my sister gets a little better, and then she gets sick all over again.

Let me tell you how I got this job at Story Workshop. It was announced over the radio that they were looking for actors, so my parents brought me over. I had to audition. There was a long, long queue of people who wanted to be in the plays, both grown-ups and children. I had to stand in the queue for a very long time. They gave us three pages of the play to read. I got the job over all the others.

This is my first day on the radio. I wasn't nervous at my audition, and I'm not nervous now.

I just know I'll be good.

Our children, our blessings, our future

Conclusion

We can't yet cure AIDS, but we know how to prolong the lives of people who are HIV-positive and increase their quality of life. We have enough resources in the world to properly care for the children left behind by AIDS—once we decide as a world community that this is what we want to do.

AIDS is preventable. We know how to create a world where girls and women have the economic power and self-esteem necessary to speak out for their own safety; where men and boys know that to be a man is more about wisdom than conquest.

It was an honor to sit with these children, to be trusted with their stories, and to get a glimpse into their lives. Months later, as this book is about to go to press, I recall their voices and think about what they taught me.

This is what life is about: it's about finding people to love and people to love us. It's about learning old ideas and coming up with new ideas of our own. It's about finding work that contributes. It's about enjoying momentary comforts, as many laughs as possible, and going to sleep with hope in our hearts for the days ahead.

This is what it is to be human: it's about knowing that other humans are just as we are. It's about shouting our stories, singing our songs, and letting them float out into the universe. It's about celebrating all our stories, all our songs, and all our histories.

We are all in this together. And that is indeed something worth celebrating.

WHAT AIDS IS AND WHAT IT DOES

- AIDS (Acquired Immunodeficiency Syndrome) is caused by the Human Immunodeficiency Virus (called HIV).

- When the presence of HIV is found in someone's blood, they are said to be HIV-positive.

- When HIV enters the bloodstream, it starts to attack the white blood cells known as T-cells. This weakens the immune system—a protective mechanism of the body that keeps us healthy.

- HIV is considered to be full-blown AIDS when the immune system becomes severely damaged. This allows certain diseases, like tuberculosis (TB), to settle in the body without resistance by the body's natural defenses.

- Other diseases AIDS patients get are pneumocystis carinii pneumonia (PCP) and a cancer of the blood vessels, called Kaposi's Sarcoma (KS).

HOW TO CATCH AIDS

There are four ways people can catch AIDS:

- unprotected sexual contact with someone who is HIV-positive
- sharing needles or syringes with someone who is HIV-positive
- receiving a blood transfusion with HIV-contaminated blood (the blood supply is now screened to make sure this no longer happens)
- a baby can be infected by an HIV-positive mother, before or during birth, or from breastfeeding.

HOW NOT TO CATCH AIDS

People cannot catch AIDS from:

- hugging someone who is HIV-positive, or playing, sharing a bathroom, sharing a drinking glass, or going to school with someone who is HIV-positive
- providing health care to someone who is HIV-positive
- having a teacher who is HIV-positive
- eating food prepared by someone who is HIV-positive

AIDS AROUND THE WORLD

- There are now 42 million people living with AIDS around the world.

- War helps spread AIDS by forcing millions of people from their homes and destroying normal family life.

- Worldwide only 5% of people who need AIDS drugs get them; only 1% of people in Africa get the AIDS drugs they need.

- Life expectancy (how long people are expected to live) has dropped across the whole of Sub-Saharan Africa from 62 to 47. In many countries, it is even lower (Zambia, 33; Swaziland, 36; Malawi, 38).

- Half of all those who are now aged 15 in Zambia are expected to die of AIDS.

- In China, AIDS has spread mostly through contaminated blood.

- In China, by 2003, there were 2 million people with HIV/AIDS; this could rise to 10-15 million by 2010.

- Nearly 70% of HIV sufferers in China are intravenous drug users.

- In 2003, there were 4 million people in India living with HIV/AIDS.

- A family in India spends half of its income caring for the person with HIV/AIDS.

- In Russia, AIDS is mostly spread through heroin users who share needles. Heroin first came into Russia during war with Afghanistan.

- Around 700,000 people in Russia have HIV/AIDS. This number is expected to rise to 8 million by 2010. Nearly all cases are intravenous drug users.

- In 2001, there were 363,000 people with HIV/AIDS in the United States; half were African Americans.

- By 2002, more than 168,000 African Americans had died from AIDS; 64% of them were women.

AIDS TERMS

Anonymous testing—A method of getting tested for HIV without giving a name.

CMV Retinitis—A virus that can damage the retina, leading to blindness if untreated. People with weak immune systems, such as those with HIV, are more susceptible to CMV.

HIV Antibody Test—A test that tells if someone is infected with HIV. Also called the AIDS Test, it is done by drawing blood. It can take up to three months before the virus produces antibodies that will show up in the test. A negative (or not infected) result should be followed up three months later by another test.

HIV-negative—Someone who, after testing, is found not to be infected with HIV.

HIV-positive—Someone who has been infected with HIV.

Immune system—A system that protects the body from foreign substances and destroys infected cells.

Opportunistic infections—Diseases that infect people with weak immune systems, such as people with HIV.

PCP, Pneumocystis carinii pneumonia—A disease that affects the lungs, a form of pneumonia. People who are HIV-positive are more likely to get PCP.

T-cell—White blood cells that turn on the immune system.

T-cell count—A way of measuring the immune system. A healthy person has a T-cell count between 600 and 1200. A person with HIV will often have a much lower count. A count below 200 is considered very serious. Also known as CD4-count.

TB, Tuberculosis—A bacterial infection that is spread through the air and usually attacks the lungs. It can also attack the bones, kidney, stomach, or lymph nodes. Being HIV-positive makes someone much more susceptible to TB.

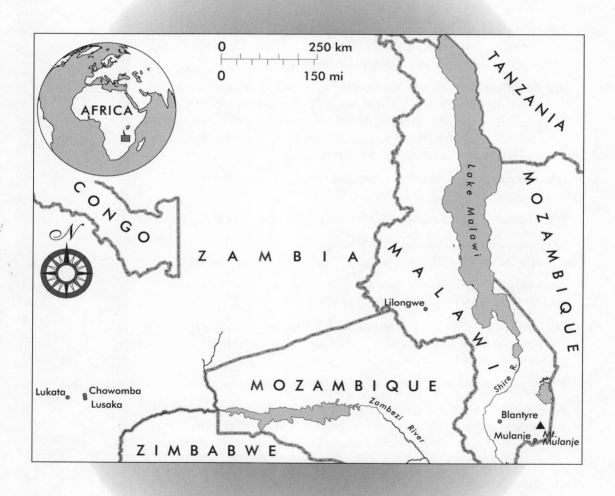

RESOURCES

BOOKS

Geballe, Shelly. *Forgotten Children of the AIDS Epidemic.* New Haven: Yale University Press, 1995.

Guest, Emma. *Children of AIDS: Africa's Orphan Crisis.* London: Pluto Press, 2001.

Kitteredge, Mary. *Teens With AIDS Speak Out.* New York: Julian Messner Publishers, 1991.

Levenson, Jacob. *The Secret Epidemic—The Story of AIDS and Black America.* New York: Pantheon Books, 2004.

Shereen Usdine, *The No-Nonsense Guide to HIV/AIDS.* Oxford: New Internationalist Publishers, 2003.

White, Ryan. *Ryan White: My Own Story.* New York: Penguin Putnam, 1992.

ORGANIZATIONS

ACT Up (AIDS Coalition to Unleash Power) 332 Bleecker St., Suite G5, New York, NY, 10014, U.S.A.; **www.actupny.org**

Friends of Mulanje Orphans, 29 Liverpool Old Rd., Walmer Bridge, Preston, Lancashire, England, PR4 5QA; **www.fomo.co.uk**

The Global Fund to Fight AIDS, Tuberculosis, and Malaria, Geneva Secretariat 53, Avenue Louis-Casaï, 1216 Geneva-Cointrin, Switzerland; **www.theglobalfund.org**

GNP+ (The Global Network of People Living with AIDS) GNP+ Central Secretariat, P.O. Box 11726, 1001 GS, Amsterdam, The Netherlands; **www.gnpplus.net**

Kairos, Canadian Ecumenical Justice Initiatives, 129 St. Clair Ave. West, Toronto, Ontario, Canada, M4V 1N5; **www.kairoscanada.org**

Stephen Lewis Foundation, 260 Spadina Avenue, Suite 501, Toronto, Ontario, Canada, M5T 2E4; **www.stephenlewisfoundation.org**

Story Workshop, Smythe Rd., Sunnyside, Private Bag 266, Blantyre, Malawi **www.storyworkshop.org**

United Nations Children's Fund (UNICEF) UNICEF House, 3 United Nations Plaza, New York, NY, 10017, U.S.A.; **www.unicef.org**

World Vision, P.O. Box 9716, Federal Way, WA 98063-9716, U.S.A.; **www.worldvision.org**

Index

A

Acquired Immunodeficiency Syndrome *see* AIDS
Africa, 1, 49
    orphans, 15, 37
    poverty, 1
    street children, 33
AID Yourself, 76
AIDS, 49, 91-92, 96
    around the world, 98
    catching, 91-92, 97
    and girls, 57
    and orphans, 14
    and poverty, 1
    signs and symptons, 52
    spreading, 70
    talking about, 58, 68-69, 91,
        93
    and teenagers, 70
    testing, 56, 88-89, 99
    and the world community, 95
Anglican Voices Choir, 85-87
anonymous testing, 99
anti-AIDS clubs, 69, 73-74
Asia, orphans, 14

B

babies, 45, 46
    HIV-positive, 48
beer, 82
Blantyre, Malawi, 25
boys, 26-27, 30
    Mpemba Boys Home, 34-37

C

catching AIDS, 91-92, 97
children
    and beatings, 90-91
    child labor, 10, 74
    prostitutes, 33
    street children, 25, 26-27, 30-32, 33
    see also babies; teenagers
Children in Crisis, 11, 12
China, 98

Chisomo Youth Center, 25, 28, 30-31, 32
Church of Central African Presbyterian (CCAP),
    67
CMV Retinitis, 99
coffins, 59
counseling, 53-56

D

death, 14, 63, 65

E

education, 60, 89
Edusport, 75-76
Ethiopa, 15

F

Friends of Mulanje Orphans, 16-17

G

games, 93-94
    see also sports
girls, 89
    and AIDS, 57
    empowerment, 75
    and sports, 76-78
Go Sister!, 75
grandmothers, 47-48

H

HIV *see* Human Immunodeficiency Virus
hospitals, 28, 49, 64-65
Human Immunodeficiency Virus (HIV), 96
    and babies, 48
    HIV Antibody Test, 99
    HIV-negative, 99
    HIV-positive, 99
    and women, 57
hunger, 31

I

immune system, 99
India, 98
infection, opportunistic, 99

K
Kaposi's Sarcoma (KS), 96
Kara Counseling Center, 53-56
Kicking AIDS Out, 75

L
labor, child, 10, 74
life expectancy, 98
Lukata, Zambia, 11
Lusaka, Zambia, 2, 53

M
malaria, 10
Malawi, 8, 10, 16, 59, 69
    radio plays, 90-94
    Scottish settlers, 67
Maula Prison Farm, 26, 38-44
measles, 77
medicine, 28, 98
men, 57, 73-74, 89
Mount Mulanje, 8, 16
Mpemba Boys Home, 34-37
Mulanje Town, Malawi, 8, 79
music, 80-81
    Anglican Voices Choir, 85-87
    singing, 15, 63-64, 82-87

N
National Association of People with AIDS,
    Malawi (NAPAM), 59-65
National Measles Campaign, 77
nsima, 4, 16-17

O
orphans, 15, 37, 83

P
peer counseling, 53-56
pneumonia, pneumocystis carinii, 96, 99
post-traumatic stress, 37
poverty, 1
    and child labor, 10
POWER, 75-76
prison, 26, 34, 38-44
    and women, 38
prostitutes, child, 33

R
radio, 90-94
rights, 88-89
robbery, 30, 84
Russia, 98

S
sexual abuse, 55
shame, 58, 68, 69-70
sickle-cell anemia, 14
singing, 15, 63-64, 82-87
sports, 75-78
stigma, 58, 69-70
Story Workshop, 90-94
street children, 25, 26-27, 30-32
    statistics, 33

T
T-cell, 99
T-cell count, 99
teachers, 37
teenagers, 70-71, 88-89
testing for HIV/AIDS, 56, 88-89
    anonymous testing, 99
    HIV Antibody Test, 99
Trendsetters Newspaper, 87-88
tuberculosis (TB), 50, 76, 99

U
United States, 98

W
women, 89
    and AIDS, 57
work *see* labor
world community, 95

Y
Youth Watch Society, 38

Z
Zambia, 2
    orphans, 15
Zimachitika, 90

About the author

Deborah Ellis is the internationally acclaimed author of a number of award-winning titles for children, including the *Breadwinner trilogy*, *A Company of Fools*, and *The Heaven Shop*. A peace activist and humanitarian field worker, Deborah has traveled the world to meet with and hear the stories of, children marginalized by poverty, war, and illness. She is the recipient of the Governor General's Award, the Jane Addams Children's Book Award, the Vicky Metcalf Award for a body of work, and the Children's Africana Book Award Honor Book for Older Readers. Raised near Paris, Ontario, Deborah lives in Simcoe, Ontario.

Photograph by Fortunato Aglialoro